# GIFTED
## BETTER LATE
## THAN NEVER

# GIFTED
## BETTER LATE THAN NEVER

MARILYN KAYE

KINGFISHER
NEW YORK

## KINGFISHER
### LONDON & NEW YORK

Text copyright © 2009 by Marilyn Kaye

Published in the United States by Kingfisher,
175 Fifth Avenue, New York, NY 10010
Kingfisher is an imprint of Macmillan Children's Books, London.
All rights reserved.

Distributed in the U.S. by Macmillan, 175 Fifth Avenue, New York, NY 10010
Distributed in Canada by H.B. Fenn and Company Ltd.,
34 Nixon Road, Bolton, Ontario L7E 1W2

Library of Congress Cataloging-in-Publication Data
has been applied for.

ISBN: 978-0-7534-6300-0

Kingfisher books are available for special promotions and premiums.
For details contact: Special Markets Department,
Macmillan, 175 Fifth Avenue, New York, NY 10010.

For more information, please visit www.kingfisherpublications.com

Printed in the U. K. by CPI Mackays, Chatham ME5 8TD
3 5 7 9 10 8 6 4 2

*For my friends who first heard this story on the beach at Bandol: Thomas and Augustin Clerc; Emilie and Marion Grimaud; Jeanne, Angèle, and Baptiste Latil; Liona, Fanny, and Alice Lutz—je vous embrasse!*

# CHAPTER ONE

JENNA KELLEY STOOD AT her bedroom window and gazed outside without really seeing anything. Not that there was much to see—just another dull brick building, exactly like her own. Sometimes, if people left their curtains open, Jenna could see people moving around in their apartments, but they rarely did anything worth watching.

Without being able to see it, she knew there was another identical structure just beyond the one opposite. Together, the three buildings made up Brookside Towers, the low-income housing development where she'd moved with her mother two years before, when she was 11. It was a pretty dreary place, but it was home, and she wasn't thrilled with the prospect of leaving it. The gray sky and steady rain outside did nothing to improve her mood.

She turned away from the window and went to her chest of drawers. Taking up a stubby black pencil, she added another layer to the already thick line that circled her eyes and stepped back to admire the effect. Kohl-rimmed eyes, short spiked hair, black T-shirt, black jeans . . . No tattoos or piercings yet, but she had a stick-on fake diamond on her right nostril, and it looked real. She hoped the way she looked would startle—maybe even shock—whomever she might be meeting.

In the mirror, behind her own reflection, she could see the empty suitcase lying open on her bed. Ignoring it, she left the room.

The sound of her footsteps on the bare floor echoed in the practically empty apartment. The silence gave her the creeps. She'd spent time alone here before, of course, but she'd always known that her mother would show up before too long. This time it was different. Her mother would be staying in the hospital rehab center for two weeks. Just knowing this made Jenna feel even more alone.

She considered turning on the TV for some companionship but then remembered that all she'd hear would be static and the screen would be a blur. Her mother hadn't paid the cable bill for three months, and the service had been cut off a while ago.

Instead, she went into the kitchen and opened the refrigerator door, even though she knew there wouldn't be anything edible inside. She removed a half-empty bottle of soda. There was no fizz left in it, but it was better than nothing, and she sat down at the rickety kitchen table to drink it.

What was her mother doing right now? she wondered. Screaming at a nurse? Demanding a gin and tonic? Jenna wanted to be optimistic. Maybe her mother would make it this time, but she couldn't count on it. Her mom had tried to stop drinking before but had never made it beyond a day or two. That very morning, before she'd left, she'd drained what was left in a bottle and then announced that this was the last alcohol she'd ever drink. Jenna had tried to read her mind, to get a more accurate picture of how serious and committed her mother was this time, but she couldn't get inside.

It was funny, when Jenna considered how easily she read minds. Young or old, male or female, smart or stupid—most people couldn't stop her from eavesdropping on their private thoughts. But there were some who were just not accessible. Like her mother.

She used to think her mother's mind was too cloudy and messed up to penetrate. Then she thought that maybe there was another reason, like a blood connection, that prevented her from reading the mind of a family member. Unfortunately, there were no other family members around, so she couldn't test that theory. She'd never known her father—according to her mother, he'd taken off before Jenna was even born. She had no brothers or sisters, and her mother had left her own family when she was young, so Jenna had never met any grandparents, aunts, uncles, or cousins.

One thing made her doubt that her inability to read her mother's mind was caused completely by the family connection. Just six months ago, when she'd been placed in the special so-called gifted class at Meadowbrook Middle School, she found that she couldn't read the mind of the teacher, a woman they called Madame. She'd tried and tried, but she was completely blocked from getting inside the teacher's head, and she'd finally given up. Maybe it was because Madame knew all their gifts so well that she was somehow able to protect herself from the special students. Gifts . . . It was a strange way to describe their unique abilities, Jenna thought. She certainly didn't feel gifted.

Having finished the flat soda, she got up and went back to her room. The suitcase on her bed reminded her that she still had a lot to do. She just didn't feel like doing it. Resolutely, she looked away and concentrated on the room that she would be bidding farewell to for at least the next two weeks.

She liked her room, and she'd spent a lot of time making it into a special place for herself—her own private, cozy cave, where she could close the door and shut out the sounds of her mother and her friends partying. The walls were a muddy gray color. She would have preferred them to be black, but beggars couldn't be choosers—the paint had been free. She'd found half-empty cans of black and white paint left on the ground behind a Dumpster, and mixing them together had given her enough to cover the walls. A dog-walking job for a neighbor had given her the resources to buy a black bedspread printed with white skulls as well as matching curtains. There were two vampire-movie posters— one showed the vampire attacking a woman, while the other was a close-up of the vampire himself with blood dripping from his mouth. And just after last Christmas, someone in her building had thrown away a perfectly good set of twinkling lights, with only a few broken bulbs. She'd arranged some garland around her door, and when she turned off the overhead light and turned on the twinkling ones, it was nicely spooky.

What kind of room would she be sleeping in tonight? A basement dungeon? Somewhere pink and white, with ruffled curtains and shelves holding a variety of Barbies? She couldn't decide which would be worse. Both images made her shudder.

Her sad fantasy was interrupted by a knock at the front door, and she groaned. For one fleeting moment, she considered not going to the door and pretending that no one was home. Eventually her visitor would go away.

Only, what was the point? She knew who was standing just outside the door, and she knew the woman wouldn't give up so easily. Even if she went away, she'd only come back, possibly with a police officer or some other official type. And they'd break down the door to get in if they had to. There was probably a law. People who were Jenna's age weren't allowed to live alone, not even for two weeks.

There was another series of knocks, more insistent this time. Reluctantly, Jenna headed to the door. She opened it to see a woman dressed in a tan suit, her fair hair pulled back neatly in a bun. The briefcase in her hand completed her professional look, and she offered Jenna a practiced smile.

"Hello, Jenna. Are you ready to go?"

"No," Jenna replied, knowing full well how rude she sounded and not caring at all. "I haven't even started packing."

The woman's expression didn't change, but now her smile looked a little strained. "Well, perhaps you'd better get going. You won't need much, you know. It's for only two weeks."

"Yeah, whatever," Jenna muttered. Two weeks in a

house full of strangers. It might as well be forever. She left the social worker and went back to her bedroom. As she began tossing whatever caught her eye into the suitcase, her thoughts went back to the two temporary foster homes that she'd stayed in before.

She was eight when her mother broke her leg in a drunken fall. If Jenna had known what was going to happen, she might have left her to recover at home instead of calling an ambulance. Social services came for her while she waited in the emergency room. She was placed in a house owned by a woman who took in children for the money that the state paid her to keep them. The woman wasn't exactly cruel—she didn't whip her or anything like that—but she basically ignored Jenna and the two other little girls who were there. It really wasn't so bad compared with the second home she went to, when she was 11 and her mother was arrested for drunk driving.

She wasn't whipped there either. She was stuck in a family of do-gooders who were constantly asking her how she was feeling and encouraging her to express her true emotions. She supposed they were trying to be kind, but Jenna could read their pity, and she would have preferred to have been beaten.

Who knew what she would be stuck with this time? Glumly, she contemplated worst-case scenarios, like religious fanatics or vegetarians. Which would be worse—going to church twice a day or being deprived of Big Macs for two weeks? As she dragged her suitcase into the living room, she decided to take a quick scan of the social worker's mind, on the off chance that she might be thinking about the place where she was about to take her. Jenna wasn't hopeful—the poor woman was probably brooding over the crummy job she had, dragging miserable kids off to foster homes.

But she was in luck—Jenna read her destination loud and clear. And when she realized where she'd be spending the next two weeks, her mood improved considerably.

"Wait a second," she told the social worker. She ran back into her room and grabbed the old stuffed animal off her bed. She hadn't packed him because she was afraid that the people at the foster home would mock her for still sleeping with a teddy bear.

Or worse, there could be some little kids at the home who would put their grubby hands all over him. Now that she knew where she was going, she could stuff him in the outside pocket of the suitcase, because he'd be safe. And so would she.

Outside the building, as they got into the car, the woman looked at her suspiciously, and Jenna didn't have to read her mind to know why. She probably expected Jenna to be whining and complaining. Her sudden passive acceptance of her fate was making the social worker nervous. Maybe she thought Jenna planned to jump out of the car at the first red light and make an escape. As they approached a stop sign, Jenna couldn't resist edging toward the car door, just to see the look of alarm on the woman's face. But she stayed put until the social worker turned onto a familiar street and pulled into a driveway.

"You've been here before, haven't you?" the woman asked, but Jenna didn't bother to respond. She hopped out of the car and waved to the girl who was standing on the front steps of the house.

Tracey Devon ran toward her. Jenna took a step backward, but to her relief, Tracey stopped short and didn't envelop Jenna in a hug. Clearly, she knew Jenna well enough to realize she wasn't the huggy type.

"Surprise!" Tracey yelled. "No, I take that back; you're not surprised at all, are you? I'll bet you read that woman's mind."

"Of course I did. Hey, how did you pull this off?"

"I just informed my parents that you needed a place to stay and I wanted you to stay here. So they called social services and made the arrangements." She took Jenna's suitcase and headed back toward the house.

*Amazing*, Jenna thought as she followed her classmate. Just a month ago, Tracey wouldn't have dreamed of asking her parents to let her have a friend stay for two weeks. And even if she'd worked up the nerve, her parents wouldn't have heard her. Nobody listened to Tracey Devon back then. Most people didn't even *see* her. Because when Tracey *felt* invisible, she actually *became* invisible, fading away whenever her emotions took over. That was Tracey's "gift"—the ability to physically disappear. Even Madame, the teacher of their gifted class, was never sure if Tracey was there or not.

The Devon parents greeted Jenna warmly.

"It's so nice to have you back with us," Tracey's father said, and Tracey's mother gave her a little hug, which Jenna managed to bear without flinching. It was hard to believe that these two friendly, welcoming parents were the same people who had been the cause of Tracey's old misery. It hadn't been on purpose—they were really sorry now, and Jenna could see that they were trying to make up for it.

"It's great to be here," Jenna replied. "I mean, compared with where I could have ended up."

And then the seven other reasons for Tracey's frequent disappearances came bounding into the room.

"Jenna!"

"Hi, Jenna!"

"Jenna, can you read us a story?"

Jenna stepped back in alarm. The septuplets were covered with spots.

"Have you ever had the measles?" Tracey asked Jenna.

"I don't know," Jenna replied honestly. She didn't remember, and if she'd had the measles when she was very young, her mother had never told her. The chances were that her mother had been so out of it that she wouldn't have noticed if Jenna had been covered with spots, and Jenna would have recovered on her own.

"It's okay—they're not contagious anymore," Tracey assured her.

Jenna tried to acknowledge their enthusiastic greetings. "Hi, Sandie, Randie, Mandie . . ." She couldn't remember the rest of the names. What was the point? The girls looked alike, and there was no way she could match each with her own name. Even the rash from their measles seemed to be in exactly the same places.

It was the birth of the septuplets five years earlier that had taken Tracey's parents' attention away from their oldest daughter. It wasn't the kids' fault—not really—but Jenna couldn't blame Tracey for having feelings toward them that weren't entirely sisterly. It was only in the past month that Tracey had begun bonding with the little girls.

"Don't bother Jenna now," Mrs. Devon reprimanded them. "She's probably tired."

"And hungry," Tracey added. "Go on up to my

room, Jenna, and I'll hunt down some munchies."

Jenna knew where Tracey's bedroom was because she'd spent a few nights there before, less than a month ago, but she wasn't sure if Tracey actually remembered that. Because Tracey hadn't really been *Tracey* the last time Jenna was there. Their "gifted" classmate Amanda Beeson had been in complete possession of Tracey's body at the time.

Plunking herself down on one of the twin beds in Tracey's room, Jenna thought about Amanda's so-called gift. She was a body snatcher, which sounded a whole lot cooler than it really was. Unfortunately for Amanda, she couldn't just snap her fingers and become an astronaut or a rock star. She could take over someone's body only if she felt sorry for that person. If she felt an abundance of sympathy for an individual, she could find herself trapped inside the wretched person's body.

Tracey had certainly been deserving of pity back then, and not just because she was fading away. She was even more pitiful when she was visible. She was scrawny—so underdeveloped that she didn't even wear a bra. Her hair was limp and stringy, her babyish clothes didn't fit properly, and she had terrible posture. She was nervous and timid, and she always looked frightened. In the eyes of someone like Amanda Beeson, who was one of the most popular girls at Meadowbrook Middle School, Tracey Devon was seriously pathetic.

Jenna knew that Amanda had been miserable stuck inside the body of a major nerd, and she doubted that Tracey had been happy about being possessed by Amanda. Strangely enough, though, it had all worked out for the best. Whether she had meant to or not, Amanda had actually helped the girl whose body she had snatched.

Tracey certainly wasn't pathetic anymore. The girl who came into the room bearing a bag of chips and a jar of guacamole bore little resemblance to the pre-Amanda Tracey. Her hair was shiny and had been cut and styled in a cute layered bob. Her eyes were bright, her shoulders were back, and her newly pierced ears held trendy gold hoops. She was still skinny, but now she took advantage of it, wearing super-slim jeans and a tight halter-top.

But the change in Tracey went far beyond her

appearance. The girl who used to be too shy to ask anyone for the time of day sat down on the twin bed where Jenna had settled herself, dumped the treats between them, and faced Jenna squarely.

"I know you don't want to talk about it, so I'm not going to ask you how you feel about your mother being in rehab. And I've told my parents not to bring up the subject either."

"Good," Jenna said, relieved.

Tracey frowned. "That's not the response I was expecting, Jenna."

"Huh?"

"Say it," Tracey ordered her.

Jenna stared at her blankly.

"Remember the magic words? *Please* and . . ."

Jenna rolled her eyes. "Okay, okay. Thank you."

Tracey nodded with approval. "See? You *can* show appreciation." Then she smiled. "Look, Jenna, I know you're grateful. You just hate to admit it because you're afraid you'll seem like Little Orphan Annie or something."

She was right, and Jenna knew it. She had a lot of pride, and she couldn't bear the idea of anyone feeling sorry for her. And saying "thank you" seemed to be like admitting that she was needy.

*This* was how Tracey had really changed. All the old hurts had created in her an ability to understand other people, to know what was really going on with them. She couldn't read minds, like Jenna, but it was as if she could read *feelings*. It wasn't exactly what Madame would call a gift, but Jenna had to admit that it was pretty interesting, and a little scary, too. Tracey was getting to know her—in spite of herself—in a way that Jenna had never allowed anyone to know her before.

Tracey tore open the bag of chips. "What do you think of my room?"

Jenna looked around. She had a vague memory of Tracey's bedroom being kind of childish and bland. Now it was decorated in bright primary colors—red curtains, red and blue plaid bedspreads, a gleaming white desk.

"Nice," she said.

"Thanks. I told my parents I wanted a completely new room, and I made them let me pick out everything myself."

"Wow!" Jenna said with admiration. "You've really got them wrapped around your little finger."

"Yeah, well, after all those years of neglect, they owed me," Tracey replied. "Hey, have you done the assignment for Monday yet?"

Her mouth stuffed with guacamole, Jenna could manage only to wrinkle her nose. That wasn't a response to the food—the guacamole was delicious—but to the reference to their homework. Madame had ordered her students to prepare a brief oral report describing when they had first become aware of their gifts.

She swallowed. "No. What about you?"

Tracey nodded. "It was easy for me. The Devon Seven were born and I was reduced to a nonentity."

"A *what*?"

"Something that doesn't exist."

That was another aspect of Tracey that was different. Once she'd started speaking up, she'd revealed something about herself that no one had ever expected—she was *smart*.

"It's not so simple for me," Jenna said. "I can't remember when I started reading minds. It seems as if I've always known what people are thinking."

"That reminds me—I've got a favor to ask." Tracey eyed her eagerly. "While you're staying here, could you *please* not read my mind?"

Jenna grinned. "Why? You got some big secret you're hiding from me?"

"No, it's just a question of privacy."

That was what Madame was always telling Jenna—that reading people's minds was like eavesdropping on private conversations or reading someone's diary.

"So do you promise you won't read my mind?"

"I don't know if I can *promise*," Jenna said. "Sometimes I can't help it. It just sort of happens. You can't control *your* gift, can you?"

Tracey sighed. "No. Ever since I got my body back from Amanda, it's harder and harder to disappear. I've been practicing, though, and I'm starting to be able to fade a little. Have you been practicing?"

"I don't need to practice. Like I said, it comes naturally."

"I mean, practice *not* mind reading. That's what

Madame means about controlling our gifts—knowing when to use them and when not to."

Jenna shrugged. "Whatever. You could try to block me. I think that's what Madame does so that I can't read her thoughts. Or . . . Wait a minute—I've got a better idea. I can't read my own mother's mind, so maybe if I think of you as a sister, I won't be able to read yours either."

"Could you do that?" Tracey asked. "Think of me as a sister?"

Jenna shifted uncomfortably. "I don't know," she replied honestly. Not being a very family-oriented person, it was hard for her to imagine the kind of feelings that sisters might have for each other. On the other hand, if she had to have a sister, she supposed Tracey would be okay.

"Yeah, all right," she relented. "I'll be your sister."

The door to Tracey's bedroom burst open and seven little Devons ran in. "Can we play now?" "Will you read to us?" "Can I have some chips?"

They were all over the place. Tracey offered Jenna a halfhearted smile. "Not that I need another one."

# CHAPTER TWO

AMANDA BEESON STRUCK a pose in front of the dressing-room mirror. "What do you think?" Personally, she didn't really care whether or not Sophie or Britney or Nina approved of the dress she was trying on—*she* thought she looked hot. But you were supposed to ask your friends for their opinions, so she did.

"So cute!" Sophie exclaimed, and Britney nodded vigorously in agreement. But Nina wasn't quite so enthusiastic.

"I don't know . . . The dress is okay, but isn't it a little too tight around your hips?"

"That's how it's supposed to be," Amanda informed her. "Figure hugging." She punctuated this with a narrow-eyed glare.

In the olden days—like, a month ago—a look like that would have reduced Nina to a quivering mass of apology. But lately, Nina hadn't been quite so easy to push around. It was almost as if she was challenging Amanda's authority as Queen Bee of the eighth grade at Meadowbrook Middle School. And this wasn't the first time.

Amanda noticed that Sophie and Britney were exchanging wary looks. She knew she needed to assert herself immediately and remind them who was in charge here. She performed a little twirl in front of the mirror and nodded in satisfaction.

"It's fabulous. It's perfect for me—I'm going to buy it," she stated firmly.

As she was making the purchase, she glanced over to where the girls were waiting for her by the door of the boutique. She couldn't hear what Nina was saying to the others, but Sophie's uneasy expression and Britney's quick glances in her direction worried her. As she handed over her mother's credit card, for the zillionth time she made a silent vow that the recent change in her life would not disrupt her social standing.

Leaving the boutique, the girls made their way through the mall and down an escalator to the food court, where eight different kinds of fast-food counters offered lunch.

"Let's get pizza," Nina declared.

Sophie and Britney looked at Amanda. Amanda took her time, letting her gaze move from the Chinese noodle place to the Burger King and beyond. "I'm going to the salad bar," she announced.

There was no reason why they couldn't each have whatever kind of food they wanted, since all the customers had to take their food away from the counters to the tables set up in the middle of the court. But it was traditional for the group to buy their lunch together as well as eat it together, and Amanda was gratified to see Sophie and Britney following her to the salad bar. A few seconds later, Nina joined them, too. Amanda mentally racked up another point for herself.

But Nina hadn't given up. As soon as they sat down at a table with their salads, she asked the question that Amanda had been expecting—and dreading.

"How's your new class?" she inquired. "What's it called—'gifted'?"

Amanda chewed slowly on a carrot stick. Eventually, however, she had to swallow and reply.

"Fine." She knew that wouldn't be a sufficient answer for Nina, and she was right.

"Why do they call it 'gifted'?" Nina wanted to know. "I mean, no offense, Amanda, but you're not a genius."

"Actually, I don't have the slightest idea why people call it that," Amanda replied casually. "The students aren't *brilliant* or anything."

Nina persisted. "But you must be special in some way to get picked for the class. Like special ed."

Amanda stiffened. *Special ed* was the term used for classes attended by kids who weren't able to do the same work as their classmates. "No, it's nothing like that."

"But you're together as a group, so you must have something in common. Let's see . . . isn't Emily Sanders in that class?"

Britney gasped. "Emily Sanders, the space cadet? The Queen of Cloud Nine?"

Sophie giggled. "She's in my biology class, and she's so out of it. Every time the teacher calls on her, she practically jumps out of her seat. It's like she's on another planet."

Amanda almost smiled. If only they knew! When Emily looked as though she was daydreaming, she was actually having visions of the future.

Nina's eyes glittered. "So, what do you have in common with Emily Sanders, Amanda?"

"Nothing," Amanda replied sharply.

"Who else is in the class?" Nina continued. "Oh yeah, that nasty boy in the wheelchair—what's his name?"

Sophie supplied it. "Charles Temple. Is he as mean as he looks, Amanda?"

"How should I know? I've never even spoken to him." But all three of them were looking at her curiously now, so she had to come up with something to explain the group. "Look, as far as I can tell, we're just a bunch of students who were picked by chance—like out of a hat. I think they're doing a study or a survey, something like that."

"Who?" Nina asked.

"What?"

"Who's doing this survey?"

Amanda groaned. "I don't know! Mr. Jackson, maybe."

"The principal?"

"Or—or the board of education, or something like that. For crying out loud, who cares?" It was definitely time to change the subject. "Hey, did you see *American Idol* last night? I can't believe Joshua was voted off—he was my favorite."

Naturally, Nina picked up on this as another opportunity to disagree with Amanda. "He wasn't a very good singer."

"But he was so cute," Sophie said. "I just love blond-haired boys with dreadlocks."

Amanda breathed a silent sigh of relief as the TV show became the topic under discussion. She couldn't really blame her friends for being curious. After all, it didn't make sense. Amanda Beeson was cool. The gifted class was mysterious. Mysterious wasn't cool. Amanda Beeson was in the gifted class. Therefore, Amanda Beeson wasn't cool. Which just went to show how sometimes logic didn't make any sense. Amanda Beeson not cool? It was a completely unthinkable conclusion.

There was no way on earth that she was going to reveal the real reason for the gifted class—it was just too embarrassing. Very few people knew why the class existed, and the class members hoped to keep it that way. Who would want the whole world to know you're a freak?

Amanda herself still couldn't believe that *she'd* been classified as one. Okay, she'd always known she was a little different. She'd been having weird experiences since she was five years old, when she saw a shabby woman begging on a street corner. She'd felt so sad for the woman that somehow her mind took over the woman's body and she actually *felt* her suffering. It happened other times, too. Whenever she experienced a lot of sympathy for another person, she *became* that person. It was very annoying.

It wouldn't be so bad, being a body snatcher, if she could pick and choose the bodies she snatched. Unfortunately, she couldn't snap her fingers and become Miss Teen America. She had to feel pity first. And it wasn't as if she could feel sorry for someone like what's-her-name, who won the gold medal for figure skating in the last Olympics. Instead, Amanda became a girl who was hurt in an accident, a battered housewife, a boy who was picked on by bullies. Or Tracey Devon.

Yeah, it was all pretty strange, but she didn't believe she belonged in that class of weirdos. She hadn't body snatched since Tracey, and as long as she could keep herself from feeling sorry for anyone, she'd never have another experience like that again. If only she could convince Madame of that and get herself released from the World of Wackos . . .

Her thoughts were interrupted by Britney's soft shriek. "Ohmigod! Don't turn around—it's Ken Preston."

Naturally, Sophie ignored Britney's direction and turned. "He is *hot*," she remarked.

No one was going to argue with that—not even Nina. When a guy was tall and broad shouldered, when he had silky sandy-blond hair falling into emerald green eyes, a cute dimple, and a square jaw, he was highly desirable. He'd been a star of the Meadowbrook soccer team until he'd had some sort of accident a couple of months before, but he still looked like an athlete—and that was what counted.

Amanda watched him with interest. He hadn't noticed the girls, but if he continued walking in the same direction, he'd go straight past their table. Oh yes, Ken Preston was very hot and totally sought after by every girl at Meadowbrook Middle School. And Ken Preston was in the gifted class, too, along with Emily Sanders and Charles Temple and Amanda Beeson.

As he got closer, the girls automatically looked away from him and toward one another. When he was practically alongside them, Nina spoke loudly. "Anyone want my tomato?"

The voice drew his attention, but he didn't look at Nina. "Hey, Amanda."

"Hi, Ken," she replied.

He moved on, and she basked in the glow of her friends' admiration. "I think he likes you," Sophie said excitedly.

Nina rolled her eyes. "Because he said hello to her?"

"He didn't speak to *me*," Britney said mournfully.

"He came to my pool party last spring, and he doesn't even remember my name," Sophie added.

"Well, I see him every day," Amanda explained. "He's in the gifted class with me."

She was gratified to see Nina's mouth drop open. "You're kidding!"

Amanda smiled. "I'll take your tomato."

It was while she was putting salt on the tomato that she noticed two other "gifted" classmates walking across the food court. This time, however, she wanted to dive under the table to avoid their seeing her. Greeting Tracey Devon and Jenna Kelley would *not* impress her friends.

Fortunately, the two girls turned in another direction, and Amanda could breathe a sigh of relief. Okay, maybe she was being snobby and shallow, but what choice did she have? Now, more than ever, she had an image to maintain.

# CHAPTER THREE

ON MONDAY AFTER lunch, Amanda hung out alone in the restroom, brushing her hair and applying layer after layer of lip-gloss until her lips were unbearably sticky. Then she used a tissue to wipe off the gunk before starting all over again. She was killing time, something she did every day at school after lunch. She would have preferred to hang out in the cafeteria, but all students were made to leave when the bell rang, to allow the kids who had the next lunch period to find seats. So she had to spend the eight minutes before the next class in the restroom.

It wasn't only because she was reluctant to go to her next class. She wanted to time her departure from the restroom so that she would enter room 209 just as the bell was ringing. She didn't want to be late—that would mean demerits and eventually staying after school for detention. But if she arrived before the bell, she'd be available for conversation with her classmates, and that was an intolerable thought.

In other classes, she enjoyed the prebell socializing that went on. But she had no desire to communicate with any of her gifted classmates. Actually, that wasn't strictly true—she wouldn't have minded talking to Ken Preston, but he always ducked in at the last minute, too. He was probably just as humiliated to be there as she was.

Today, her timing was slightly off. When she entered the classroom, she looked at the clock and noted with dismay that there was still maybe half a minute before the bell—just enough time for Tracey Devon to turn to her and try to start a conversation.

"I just thought you'd like to know—the girls are feeling a lot better now."

Amanda looked at her blankly. "Huh?"

"The Devon Seven. My sisters." Tracey grinned. "Maybe I should say *our* sisters. Remember, I told you last week that they had the measles."

"Oh yeah, right," Amanda said while thinking,

*Please, bell, ring now.*

"They've got only a couple of spots each," Tracey went on.

"That's nice," Amanda mumbled, refusing to meet Tracey's eyes. Finally, the bell rang, and no one could talk.

Amanda would never admit it to Tracey—or anyone else, for that matter—but she was actually sort of interested in the well-being of the septuplets. When she'd lived inside Tracey's body, she had almost enjoyed the time she spent with the cute little girls. But that was then and this was now, and as far as Amanda was concerned, all connections were severed when she got back to being her own self again.

Would Tracey never give up? she wondered. Just because Amanda had inhabited her body for a while, Tracey seemed to think that she and Amanda should have some sort of special bond. Ever since the girl had recovered her body, she'd been acting like they were friends—as if!

True, Tracey wasn't anywhere near as nerdy as she used to be before Amanda so kindly made her over. But she certainly wasn't in Amanda's league, and with her own status on the line, Amanda couldn't afford to be seen as friendly with Tracey Devon.

It was the same with Jenna Kelley. When she had been Tracey, Amanda had been forced to befriend Jenna. And okay, maybe she did find the rebellious girl a teeny-weeny bit interesting. But Jenna wasn't any higher on the popularity chain than Tracey—neither of them was even remotely cool—and Amanda was in no position to be charitable.

Madame had risen from her desk and was calling for attention. The petite, dark-haired woman gazed over the class like a shepherd overseeing a flock—kindly but watchful.

"On Friday I asked you to try to recall the moment when you first became aware of your gift," she said. "Would anyone like to volunteer to go first?"

Why did she bother to ask that? Amanda wondered. That was one way in which this class was no different from any other class—nobody ever volunteered.

Madame sighed. "You will all have to report sooner or later."

But everyone preferred not starting, and Madame

gave up. "Charles, you can go first. When did you first realize you had a gift?"

All eyes turned apprehensively to the boy in the wheelchair. When Charles was asked to do something he didn't want to do, he could get upset. And when Charles was upset, he could create a tornado in the classroom. Not only would he make a mess, but there was always the possibility that he would send a freshly sharpened pencil into someone's eye. It hadn't happened yet, but everyone knew it *could*.

But Madame had been working with Charles on controlling his temper, and it seemed to have had some effect. Charles didn't look happy, but at least the clock didn't drop off the wall, the light bulbs didn't explode, and he actually attempted to answer the question.

"I'm not exactly sure. I think I could always make things move. My mother says that when I was a baby and I was hungry, I could make the bottle come to me in my crib."

"But when's the first time you remember using your gift?" Madame asked.

Charles went into a long, rambling tale,

something about ruining his older brother's baseball game by sending every ball he hit directly into the pitcher's mitt. Bored, Amanda wondered for the zillionth time why Madame made them talk so much about their stupid gifts. What was the point?

The teacher was always telling them that if they discussed their gifts, they would come to understand them, and if they understood them, they could learn to control them. Maybe some of the other kids needed to talk, but Amanda knew perfectly well how to control her "gift"—which she didn't consider a gift at all, but something more like a bad habit. All she had to do was avoid caring about anyone other than herself and she'd never run the risk of snatching anyone's body. Instead of feeling sorry for people, she made fun of them.

Once in a while, she'd be struck with a pang of guilt when she mocked a classmate. But whenever that happened, all she had to do was recall the awfulness of waking up as Tracey Devon and the mean comments spilled out pretty easily.

Charles had finally finished his story, and Madame called on Sarah Miller next. Given Sarah's very special gift and the fact that she never demonstrated it, Amanda was actually curious to hear what she had to say. With her pretty heart-shaped face and short black curly hair, Sarah looked so sweet that it was hard to believe she had the most dangerous gift of all.

She was such a good student that she'd actually prepared notes for her report, and she consulted them now before she spoke.

"I was six years old, and my parents were fighting a lot. They weren't violent or anything like that—they just argued—but they were loud. One night they went on and on and on, and I kept thinking, *Stop, stop, stop* . . . And they did."

Madame raised her eyebrows. "Couldn't that have been a coincidence?"

Sarah looked sheepish. "Maybe . . . except just having them be quiet wasn't enough for me. When I realized what I could do, I made them hug each other. Then I sent my mother to the kitchen to make popcorn, and I made my father turn on the TV, and I had us all curl up together on the couch to watch *The Wizard of Oz*."

Charles spoke up. "Wow! You are so lucky. I can only make *things* move. You can make people do what you want them to do."

Amanda didn't think that Sarah looked as if she felt lucky. Madame must have been thinking the same thing, because she looked at Sarah with an expression that was unusually sympathetic.

"Were you happy about this?" Madame asked quietly.

"At first . . . and then I got scared. Because when I realized what I could do . . ." She shivered and looked pleadingly at the teacher. "Do I have to keep on talking about this?"

"No, that will be enough," Madame said. "For now. Emily, when did you first realize you could see the future?"

Emily didn't look like she particularly wanted to talk either. She took off her glasses, cleaned them with a cloth, and put them back on. Then she started twisting a lock of her long, straight brown hair as she mumbled something.

"Speak up, Emily," the teacher said.

The girl's voice was only slightly louder. "I talked

about this in class before."

"Tell us again," Madame said. Her voice was kind but firm. Amanda couldn't believe she was going to force poor Emily to tell that dreary story again. Even *she* had to admit that it was pretty depressing. Did Madame really think this would make Emily feel better about her gift?

Emily did as she was told. "I was really little, only five. It was in the morning, and my father was just about to leave for work. I remember that he wore a suit and carried a briefcase. I had a vision that he was going to be hit by a car just in front of our house, and I didn't tell him. And he was struck by a speeding car and was killed."

Amanda could see the tears forming behind Emily's thick glasses. Despite herself, she felt sorry for the girl, and she became nervous. She had to do or say something right away or she might find herself inside that spacy girl's body.

"You shouldn't feel bad," she declared quickly. "I mean, it's not like it was your fault."

"I feel guilty that I didn't tell him about the vision," Emily said.

Amanda waved a hand in the air as if to brush that notion aside. "Get over it. Like you said yourself, it was the first time you had a vision. You couldn't have known you were seeing the future."

Emily whispered something.

"Speak up, Emily," Madame said again.

"What if . . . what if it wasn't the first time?"

Madame looked interested. "What do you mean?"

"I keep thinking . . . maybe I had visions before that. Like I remember one day, my mother said she was going to bake a cake, and in my mind I saw a burned cake, and she forgot to take it out of the oven, and it did burn. And another time, I could see the people who would be living in the house next door even before it was sold . . ." Her voice was trembling now. "What if I had told my father what I could see in his future? I could have saved his life!"

Jenna spoke. "Emily, you were five years old! You didn't understand what was going on inside your head."

"You can't feel guilty about it," Tracey declared. "Even if you'd told your father that he was about to be hit by a car, what makes you think he would have believed you? Who listens to little kids making predictions?"

"They're right, Emily," Madame said. "You're not responsible for your father's death."

"I just wish I knew what *he* thinks," Emily said. Suddenly, she drew in her breath sharply, leaned forward, and tapped the shoulder of the boy sitting in front of her.

"Ken, you talk to dead people, don't you? Could you maybe try to find my father and ask him if he's mad at me? And tell him I'm sorry I didn't warn him?"

Ken's brow was furrowed as he turned around and faced her. "I don't talk to dead people, Emily. Dead people talk to me!"

"You don't talk back? I mean, haven't you ever had a conversation with one of them?"

"Are you nuts?" Ken exclaimed. "I don't want to encourage them—I want them to stop!"

Amanda listened to this exchange with interest. It was clear to her that Ken didn't like having a so-called gift any more than she did.

"But if you could just—"

"Emily!" Madame interrupted her. "This is inappropriate. As you well know, there are people out there who would want to exploit us if they knew about our gifts. *We* do not exploit one another. Ken, will you tell us about the first time a dead person spoke to you?"

Ken squirmed in his seat. "I really don't remember."

Charles stared at him in disbelief. "Oh, give me a break. You don't remember the first time you heard a dead person talking to you?"

Ken didn't look at him as he responded. "No. Um, I guess maybe they've been talking to me since I was born, so I never noticed."

Little Martin Cooper turned to Ken. "What does it feel like, hearing dead people? Is it like having ghosts inside your head?" His expression was fearful, as if he was afraid that the ghosts might suddenly pop out of Ken's head and start haunting *him*.

"It's not fun," Ken said shortly.

"Is a dead person talking to you right now, Ken?" Tracey asked.

He flinched. "Jeez, you make it sound like I'm a crazy person, hearing voices. No. Maybe. I don't know—I don't listen."

Amanda was skeptical, and she could tell that Madame didn't believe him either. Personally, she didn't care one way or another. She was too busy contemplating Ken from another angle. As a boyfriend.

Why not? He was cute, he was cool, and her friends would be impressed if she hooked up with him. Even Nina would have to show her some respect. Being with someone like Ken Preston would definitely put her back on top. And it wasn't as if *she'd* suffer in the process of creating a relationship with him . . .

"Amanda? When do you first recall experiencing your gift?"

Amanda began to tell her story about the beggar she saw when she was five. As she spoke, she kept glancing at Ken. Maybe he'd be impressed with the fact that she could feel so sorry for people. But he wasn't even paying attention.

She didn't tell the part about how she had been Tracey Devon—she couldn't bear the thought of Ken picturing the old Tracey in his mind and connecting the image with Amanda. Even the new-and-improved Tracey wasn't up to her standards.

Then Tracey's hand went up, and Amanda's stomach fell. Fortunately, it was almost time for the bell.

"We'll hear from you tomorrow, Tracey," Madame said. "And from Jenna and Martin."

"What about Carter?" Charles wanted to know.

Martin started laughing, and Madame shot him a warning look. Then she looked at the boy whom no one knew.

"Carter, will you give a report on your gift tomorrow?" she asked.

There was no response to her question, and like the others, Amanda wasn't surprised. They couldn't be sure he *had* a gift. For as long as he'd been at Meadowbrook, he hadn't spoken. No one even knew his real name. A teacher had found him wandering on Carter Street. Not only mute, but he appeared to be an amnesiac, too. He was a complete and total mystery, which meant that he was very weird, and Amanda knew that was why he'd been put in this class. With the other weirdos.

Who, in a million years, would ever believe that Amanda Beeson might have anything in common with someone like Carter Street? It was truly sickening. She had to get out of here. And it certainly wouldn't hurt to have a partner to help her plan how to make her—*their*—exit.

Her seat was closer to the door than Ken's, so when the bell rang, she hurried out and then waited for him. As soon as he emerged, she began walking alongside him and spoke casually.

"I can totally relate, Ken."

"Huh?"

"With what you said in class today. I really do understand."

He looked at her in puzzlement. "Dead people talk to you, too?"

"No—I mean, I don't want my gift either."

"Yeah, well . . ." He looked away, and she understood. The busy, crowded hallway was no place for a discussion about something so personal.

"I was thinking, maybe we could talk about it sometime," she ventured.

There was a considerable lack of enthusiasm in his expression. "Isn't that what we do every day in class?"

"Sure, but I was thinking, just you and me . . ." Her voice trailed off as he frowned. She wasn't even sure if he'd heard her.

"I gotta go," he said abruptly. And he ducked into a boys' restroom.

She supposed he might have really needed to go to the bathroom. Because why wouldn't he want to get together with her? She was pretty, she was popular—most boys would be pleased to find her flirting with them. And Ken had actually kissed her once, at Sophie's pool party the previous spring. Of course, it hadn't *meant* anything. Some other boys at the party had probably dared him to do it—they were all acting pretty goofy that day—but still . . .

Maybe he really hadn't heard her. One of those dead people could have been trying to get his attention. But that was exactly why he *should* listen to her. If she could lose *her* gift, she might be able to help him get rid of his.

Those other "gifted" kids—they were freaks. She and Ken were cool. They belonged together—and out of that class.

# CHAPTER FOUR

JENNA HAD LEFT BROOKSIDE Towers only two days before, but already the buildings looked more grim and forbidding and not like home at all. She was very glad that Tracey and Emily had offered to come along with her after school. Of course, she didn't tell them that she was grateful.

"You know, I could do this by myself," she informed them. "I don't know why you guys are tagging along."

To Emily, Tracey said, "That's Jenna's way of saying thank you."

Jenna ignored that. "And if the elevator is out of order, you'll be sorry. I'm on the fifth floor."

"You can't bring back everything by yourself," Tracey pointed out, turning to Emily. "She forgot her raincoat, her bathrobe—lots of things. Including all her school stuff."

"A Freudian slip," Emily commented.

"What's that?" Jenna asked, suspecting that it wasn't something you wore underneath your clothes.

"It's when you think you're doing something accidentally but you have a subconscious reason. Like, you *forgot* your school stuff because you don't like school."

That was one of the interesting things about Emily, Jenna thought. She might act all spacy and out of it, but then she'd come out with something really smart like that.

"And don't worry about the elevator," Emily added. "It's working."

And that was another weirdly interesting thing about Emily. "I can't believe you waste your gift predicting such stupid stuff," Jenna remarked.

"I know," Emily said mournfully. "Things like that just come to me. Then when I *try* to predict something, I get it wrong. I'm getting better, though. I got four out of seven weather forecasts right last week."

She was right about the elevator, too. But when they got off on the fifth floor, Jenna hesitated.

"What's the matter?" Tracey asked.

She couldn't tell them the truth—that she was afraid her mother had given up, had left rehab, and was now passed out on the living-room floor.

"Nothing," she said. Thank goodness *they* couldn't read *her* mind. "The apartment is at the end of the hall." Gritting her teeth, she strode forward, and the other two followed her. To her relief, the apartment was empty.

"Have you heard from your mother?" Emily asked.

Jenna shook her head as she led them into her bedroom. "People in rehab aren't allowed to be in contact with anyone on the outside. I guess she's doing all right." She heard something in Tracey's mind and turned to her. "Okay, maybe it's wishful thinking, but I can hope, can't I?"

"Hey, you promised!" Tracey exclaimed in outrage.

"Sorry, I forgot," Jenna lied. She opened her dresser drawer and began throwing stuff onto the bed.

"What are you guys talking about?" Emily wanted to know.

"Jenna promised not to read my mind while she was staying with me," Tracey told her.

"You should do what I do," Emily said.

"What do you do?" Tracey asked.

"I don't know, but Jenna never reads my mind."

Jenna grinned. "That's because I don't believe you're ever thinking anything that's worth paying attention to."

"Ha-ha, very funny." Emily picked up Jenna's slippers. "What are we going to put all this stuff in?"

Tracey produced several empty bags from her backpack, and the girls began filling them. Emily picked up a notebook and stopped.

"Are these your notes from the gifted class?"

Jenna glanced at the notebook. "Yeah. Why?"

"Because I just got a vision of our next homework assignment."

Tracey looked at her with interest. "So if you can touch something, it helps with your predictions?"

"I don't know—this has never happened before." She sighed. "There's so much I don't understand about my gift."

"Same here," Tracey said. "Now that I don't feel like a nobody, how can I make myself disappear?"

"And why can't I read everyone's mind?" Jenna

wondered. She turned to Emily. "What's the assignment? Not that I care," she added hastily. "I probably won't do it anyway."

"Madame is going to ask us to think about how we could use our gifts in a career."

"Great," Jenna groaned as she picked through her underwear in search of items without holes. "I guess I could be some kind of magician. Like, 'Think of a number and I'll tell you what it is.'"

"You could be a psychologist," Tracey suggested. "It would definitely help to know what people are thinking."

"Or a police officer," Emily said. "You'd always know when people were lying, and you could solve crimes that way."

"If I could become invisible whenever I wanted, I could be a detective," Tracey remarked. "Or a spy! That would be intense!"

"I'd like to do something that helps people," Emily mused. "If I could predict natural disasters, like earthquakes, I could warn people to move before they happen."

"No one would believe you," Jenna told her.

"You'd be like Chicken Little, running around yelling, 'The sky is falling.' Can you predict what's going to happen to me this week?"

"Let me think . . ." Emily scrunched her forehead and closed her eyes. After a moment, she said, "You're going to meet a tall, dark, handsome stranger."

Tracey started laughing. "You sound like one of those fake gypsy fortunetellers."

"No, really—I see that," Emily insisted. Then her expression changed.

"What?" Jenna asked.

"He's going to make you cry."

"Oh, puh-leeze!" Jenna snorted. "The day some stupid boy makes me cry . . . You know, Em, if I had your talent, I'd use it to become a professional gambler and make some money. Like, in horse races, I'd know who to bet on. Or I'd figure out the next winning lottery numbers."

Emily winced. "Like Serena."

"Oh, right." Jenna had almost forgotten about the awful student teacher who had tried to make Emily do exactly that. "Sorry." She turned to Tracey. "If I could be invisible, I'd follow around famous people and see how they really live. Wouldn't it be awesome to hang out with Britney Spears? Or Prince William?"

"That's not exactly a career," Tracey said, "unless you're writing a gossip column."

A sudden knock on the door made them all turn in that direction. "Are you expecting anyone?" Tracey asked Jenna.

"No." Jenna went out of the bedroom and headed to the door.

"Then don't answer it!" Tracey called.

Jenna looked through the door's peephole. Unfortunately, it hadn't been cleaned since—well, it had never been cleaned, probably. So she couldn't see much—just the fact that someone sort of tall with dark hair was standing on the other side of the door.

"Hello?" she called.

"Excuse me," replied a masculine voice. "I'm looking for Barbara Kelley."

"She's not here."

Tracey was at her shoulder. "If you don't know who it is, don't let him in," she hissed.

The man at the door must have heard her.

"Whoever said that is absolutely right. Never open the door to strangers. I'll come back another time."

The figure disappeared, and Jenna turned back to her curious friends. "Probably a bill collector," she said. "Or he's selling something. I've never seen him before."

"Did you get a good look at him?" Emily asked.

"Not really. He was tall, he had dark hair . . . Why are you grinning like that?"

"Because I was right with my prediction! You just met a tall, dark, handsome stranger."

"I couldn't tell if he was handsome," Jenna pointed out.

Emily sighed. "Well, he was tall and dark and he was a stranger. Three out of four isn't bad." Then, suddenly, her face changed and she shivered.

"*Now* what's the matter?" Jenna asked.

"I just got a bad feeling about him," Emily said. "Like maybe he's not a nice person."

"That doesn't make sense," Tracey said. "If he was a burglar or something like that, he wouldn't have told Jenna not to open the door."

"That's true," Emily admitted. "See? You can't rely

on me. I get these visions, but a lot of the time I don't understand what they mean."

"It's too bad we can't blend our gifts and work together," Tracey commented. "Jenna could read your mind and make sense out of what you see in your head."

"She can't read my mind," Emily reminded her.

"I didn't say that," Jenna argued. "I never try."

"Try now," Emily urged. "What am I thinking?"

Jenna closed her eyes and concentrated. Then she frowned. "Nothing. You're as empty as Carter Street."

Emily grinned. "I just imagined a wall in front of my thoughts."

"Ooh, let me try that!" Tracey cried out excitedly. "Jenna, try to read my mind."

"You made me promise not to."

"Well, I release you from your promise, just for one minute. Starting now."

Feeling like a circus performer, Jenna groaned, but how could she say no to someone who was putting her up for two weeks? So she closed her eyes again.

It didn't take much concentration to read Tracey's thoughts. "You're thinking about dinner tonight and hoping for spaghetti and meatballs."

Tracey made a face. "But I put up a wall, just like Emily did. A brick wall! How come it didn't work for me?"

"How should I know?" Jenna retorted. "Why are some of Emily's predictions right and others not?"

"We're mysteries," Emily said. "We're not like other people. We've got weird gifts that we don't understand, so we can't expect them to work all the time until we learn more about them."

Once again, vague, scatterbrained Emily was making an intelligent observation. They really were mysteries, all of them, Jenna thought.

And personally, she liked being a mystery. It meant that life would be full of surprises.

# CHAPTER FIVE

THE NEXT DAY, WHEN she arrived at school, Amanda went up to the principal's office. There was a student working at the reception desk—a girl named Heather who'd been in Amanda's geometry class last year. Heather wasn't a nerd, but she wasn't in the top clique either, and Amanda was pretty sure she could get Heather to do her a favor.

She was right, and after graciously accepting a compliment from Heather on her new yellow platform shoes, she left the office with a copy of Ken Preston's class schedule. Then she organized her day so that she would *accidentally* bump into him at various times between classes.

The first two times, he didn't even see her. The third time, he saw her, and when she greeted him, he said hi but didn't stop to talk. And the fourth time, when she tried to start a conversation, he claimed to be busy and hurried off.

It didn't make any sense. Was it possible—really, truly possible—that he wasn't attracted to her? It was hard to believe, but she decided she would have to explore all the possibilities of getting together with him.

For the first time since she'd started the class, she hurried to room 209. She knew Ken wouldn't be there—he always showed up at the last minute. There was someone else she wanted to see—someone who just might be able to help her connect with Ken.

Being the perfect student, Sarah was already in her seat when Amanda arrived. Whoever sat in front of her wasn't there yet, so Amanda took that seat. Sarah looked up in surprise.

"Hello, Amanda."

Amanda tried to remember if she'd ever spoken directly to Sarah. She didn't think so, but she smiled brightly and tried to act as if they talked every day.

"Hi, Sarah. How're you doing?"

Sarah recovered from her shock quickly. "Fine. How are you?"

Amanda put on a doleful face. "Not too good."

Sarah had a reputation for being sweet and understanding, and she demonstrated that now. She looked concerned. "What's the matter?"

"It's Ken," Amanda said sadly. "You know—Ken Preston, in our class."

"What's wrong with Ken?"

"Well, he's so timid . . ."

"Really? I never noticed that."

Amanda continued quickly. "Well, he is, and I know he wants to ask me out, but he's too shy. Maybe you could help him."

Sarah looked confused. "What could *I* do?"

"You've got that special ability to make people do things with your mind. And I was thinking, you could make him ask me out. Nothing major—just something like a movie or miniature golf."

Sarah just stared at her, speechless. Her eyes were very wide.

"It would just be this one time," Amanda assured her. "I'm sure once I got him alone, he'd recover from his shyness. Would you do this for me? I mean, for him?"

Sarah shook her head. "I can't, Amanda."

"Of course you can. You've got the gift!"

"I suppose I should say, 'I won't.' Amanda, my gift is dangerous. And the only way I can deal with it is to not use it at all."

"But that's silly!" Amanda exclaimed. "It's just a date. How is that dangerous?"

"That's not the point, Amanda."

Amanda frowned. She didn't care about the point. She just wanted a date.

Sarah explained, "I used to have a fantasy about going to the Winter Olympics so I could help the figure skaters not fall. But I know now that doing good deeds can be just as dangerous as doing bad deeds. Because one thing could lead to another. Do you see what I mean?"

"No. Look, Sarah, if you do this for me, we could be friends. You could sit with us at lunch." Amanda knew that her table, with Britney, Sophie, Nina, Katie, and the others, was considered the best girls' table in the cafeteria. Heather-in-the-office would *kill* for a chance to sit at that table.

But Sarah wasn't Heather-in-the-office. "I'm

sorry, Amanda. I just can't."

She sounded as if she meant it, too. Amanda rearranged her features into an expression that she hoped looked menacing. "Sarah, do you remember what my gift is?"

"Of course I do—you talked about it yesterday."

"Well, what if I took over your body and made Ken ask me out? I mean, me–Amanda, not me–you."

Sarah didn't seem the least bit frightened. "You'd have to feel sorry for me first, Amanda. And you don't, do you?"

She was right. Sarah wasn't the coolest, prettiest, or most popular girl at Meadowbrook, but there was nothing pathetic about her either. Amanda gave up on the idea of using Sarah. She'd have to find another way to reach Ken.

The others were coming in now, so she went back to her own seat. As usual, Ken came in last, and he still had that distracted expression on his face. She didn't even bother trying to catch his attention. What was she going to do? There had to be a way.

The bell rang, class started, and Madame called on Tracey to give her report. Amanda didn't bother listening—having been Tracey, she knew Tracey's story by heart. Tracey had been a happy only child, then her mother had septuplets, Tracey was ignored, she started to disappear, blah-blah-blah. Amanda spent the time doodling, trying to come up with a way to get Ken's attention. What if she went to his house, knocked on his door, and asked him to—

"Amanda?"

She looked up. "Yes, Madame?"

"Don't you have something to say to Tracey?" The teacher gazed at her sternly. "Apparently you weren't listening. Tracey was thanking you for helping her learn to assert herself."

Sarah turned to look at her with a startled expression, as if she was surprised to learn that Amanda could do something nice for someone else. Jenna was looking at her, too, and grinning—she'd known when Amanda had been inside Tracey's body because of her mind-reading skills. And she knew perfectly well that Amanda hadn't been trying to improve Tracey's life—only her own for as long as she was stuck being Tracey. But there was only one reaction Amanda was really interested in.

She looked at Ken. He was staring out the window, daydreaming, maybe, or listening to dead people, but in any case, he obviously hadn't been paying attention to Tracey's story. What a relief.

Madame was still staring at her. "Amanda?"

"Oh, yeah. Uh, that's okay. I mean, you're welcome. Whatever."

Madame called on Martin next. The boy—who looked to be at least two years younger than anyone else—spoke in a very annoying, whiny voice, which made it hard to listen to his story.

"It was a couple of years ago. I was shooting baskets in my driveway."

The thought of undersized Martin playing basketball was almost too much for Amanda to deal with, but she knew better than to show it. But neither Jenna nor Charles had her self-control, and they started laughing. Martin clenched his fists.

Madame rapped on her desk. "Stop it at once! Martin, remember your exercise. Close your eyes and count backward from ten."

Amanda half hoped that the exercise wouldn't work. She'd never actually seen Martin demonstrate his gift. It would be interesting to see if he would attack a person in a wheelchair. As for Jenna, Amanda wouldn't mind seeing her get shaken up a little.

But Martin relaxed, and the animal or whatever was inside him calmed down.

"Anyway, a couple of guys came by and said they wanted to play with me. Only they kept the ball and wouldn't let me have it. I tried to get it back, but they were bigger than me. And they laughed."

He didn't have to say more. Everyone knew what happened when Martin thought people were making fun of him.

"Did you hurt them badly?" Madame asked.

"One of them got away. I broke the other one's arm, but that was all."

"So you were able to restrain yourself," Madame commented.

"Well, not exactly. It's just that he was screaming so hard that I lost the feeling."

Supposedly, it was this "feeling" that gave Martin the strength of a bear or some other type of strong animal. In any case, his power went beyond anything a normal human being could do—even a big bodybuilder.

"And that's the first time you remember getting the feeling?" Madame asked.

"Yeah, I think so. But my mother told me that when I was three, my father took a toy away from me and I pushed him across the room. My father says she dreamed this and it never happened." He grinned. "But he never tried to take anything away from me again, so I guess he learned his lesson. I must have done a pretty good job for a three-year-old."

"This is nothing to be proud of, Martin," Madame reprimanded. "You have to learn to channel your strength and direct it appropriately."

"Maybe you could go into demolition work someday," Jenna suggested. "I'll bet you'd be great at tearing down buildings."

Martin considered this. "I'd rather tear down people."

Sarah gasped. "Martin! That's not right!"

"It's their own fault," Martin complained. "People are always picking on me. I'm small, so they think they can push me around. If they didn't pick on me, I wouldn't get the feeling and I couldn't hurt them."

"Martin, you have to take responsibility for your gift," Madame said. "We'll hear from Jenna next."

Luckily, Jenna was saved by the bell—not the usual one, but the three special chimes that signified an announcement was about to be made over the intercom. This was followed by the disembodied voice of the principal's secretary.

"Would Jenna Kelley please come to the office?"

Everyone looked at Jenna, who immediately went all defensive. "I didn't do anything!"

"Just go to the office, Jenna," Madame said. "You can give your report another day."

*Lucky dog,* Amanda thought. It was very likely that Madame would forget that Jenna hadn't given her report and would never call on her again to do it. Jenna didn't deserve the good fortune.

On the other hand, Jenna was on her way to Mr. Jackson's office. Amanda brightened. Nobody ever got called to the principal's office for a good reason.

# Chapter Six

JENNA RACKED HER BRAIN, trying to think of a reason for being called to the office so that she could come up with a story or an excuse to get out of it. She'd done plenty of bad things in her time at Meadowbrook, but she hadn't broken any major school rules recently. She hadn't been cutting classes—not for a while, anyway. She hadn't cheated on any tests lately. Come to think of it, she'd been unusually good the past couple of weeks, not even going to the mall and hanging out with Slug and Skank, the lowlife types she'd befriended on the street. She hadn't even seen them since they'd been picked up for shoplifting.

What could be so big that she'd be called out of class? Had they looked in her locker and found something bad? Okay, it was a mess, but there weren't any cigarettes or drugs or alcohol stashed away. Surely you didn't get called to the office for a couple of Kit Kat bars.

Then another possibility occurred to her, and she felt sick. Her mother . . . had something happened to her mother? Her legs turned to jelly and she stopped walking. That was definitely the kind of thing a person would be called out of class for—a family situation. Something really terrible, like an accident or . . . or worse.

Her mother. She was weak, she was an alcoholic, she'd never win any mother-of-the-year prizes, but Jenna loved her. And the thought of losing her . . .

"Jenna? Are you all right?"

The concerned voice belonged to Mr. Gonzalez, the school counselor. Jenna had been forced to have sessions with him after her stint in the juvenile detention center. He was nice enough, but she'd put so much effort into lying to him during their sessions that she couldn't tell him the truth now.

"Sure, I'm fine. I'm just on my way to, um . . ."

"The principal's office?" He smiled. "It's okay. I know all about it. If you need to talk later, you know where I am." And he ambled off.

He left Jenna gaping. He knew why she'd been called to the office, and he was *smiling*. So she couldn't be in trouble and it couldn't be anything terrible, like her mother being hurt. It had to be something else.

Then she wanted to kick herself. Why hadn't she read his mind? Then she'd already know!

She moved quickly now, down the hall, around the corner, and up the half flight of stairs to the administration wing. When she walked into the main office, the secretary recognized her, but for once she wasn't wearing a reproving look. She beamed at Jenna and picked up the phone.

"Jenna Kelley is here, Mr. Jackson." She put down the phone. "You can go right in, Jenna."

Still feeling shaky, Jenna went to the door and rapped. A familiar booming voice rang out. "Come in, Jenna."

She opened the door. The heavyset principal was behind his desk, and for the first time ever, he looked pleased to see Jenna. There were two chairs facing the principal's desk, and a man was sitting in one of them.

He turned as Jenna approached, and she thought he looked vaguely familiar. "Hello, Jenna," he said.

It was his voice that put the memory in focus. This was the man who had come to the door yesterday looking for her mother.

"Hello," she said uncertainly.

"Sit down," the principal said, and as she did, once again she became nervous. Had this strange man come to give her bad news about her mother? No, that couldn't be it. He, too, was smiling. And Emily had been right about something—he was definitely handsome.

The principal spoke. "I'd like you to meet Mr. Stuart Kelley."

Jenna's eyes darted back and forth between the principal and the strange man. *Kelley* was a pretty common name, but she had to ask.

"Are you related to me?"

The man nodded and spoke gently. "I'm your father, Jenna."

His voice was soft, and Jenna was certain that she'd misheard him. "What?"

The principal repeated, "This is your father, Jenna. He's been searching for you for—how long, Mr. Kelley?"

"A long time," the man said, smiling. "But now I've finally found you, Jenna."

Jenna narrowed her eyes. She didn't know what kind of scam this guy was trying to pull, but she wasn't about to fall for it. She turned to the principal.

"This is a mistake, Mr. Jackson. I don't have a father."

Mr. Jackson gave her a jovial smile. "Everyone has a father, Jenna, even if they don't know who he is. It takes two, you know." He uttered a hoarse laugh at his silly remark.

Jenna had never much liked the principal, and now she *really* disliked him. She stood up.

"Can I go back to my class now?" Boy, those were words she'd never expected to hear herself saying. Of course, she'd never expected to be confronted by some prankster claiming to be her father.

"Sit down, Jenna!" Mr. Jackson's tone had changed—now he was his usual authoritative self. She sat down, but she didn't look at the man. She kept her wary gaze on the principal.

"This man is your father," Mr. Jackson declared. "I have checked his credentials, and I am satisfied with the evidence he has provided."

*What evidence?* Jenna wondered, but she didn't ask. She tried to do a quick read of the principal's mind, but all she could come up with was a confirmation that Mr. Jackson didn't like her any more than she liked him.

"Look at me, Jenna," the strange man said quietly. Despite herself, she did. He had nice eyes—a deep, rich blue, like hers. But lots of people had blue eyes.

"I can understand how you feel," Stuart Kelley went on. "What I did to you and your mother—it was a terrible thing. But I wasn't a very nice person back then. I was young and restless and I didn't want any responsibilities. I loved your mother, but when she told me she was pregnant, I couldn't deal with it. I didn't have the maturity. So I left."

Jenna steeled herself to stare right back into those blue eyes. "Where did you go?"

"California." He smiled in an almost sheepish way. "I was a good-looking kid, and I thought I could make it in the movies."

Jenna eyed him skeptically. "Did you? Are you some famous movie star I've never heard of?"

He laughed. "Hardly. Did you ever see *Invasion of the Mile-High Martian Zombies*?"

Jenna shook her head.

"I don't think it was ever released in theaters. I'm pretty sure it went directly to DVD. I was one of three hundred Martian zombies on stilts. You can't pick me out because we all wore the same mask. And I didn't even get a credit. So no, I'm not a famous movie star. I'm an unknown DVD extra."

At least he was able to poke fun at himself, Jenna thought. But she'd watched enough crime dramas on TV to know that scam artists were usually charming.

"How did you know you had a daughter?" she challenged him.

"Your mother had a friend, Sylvia Tinsley. You wouldn't remember her—she passed away ten years ago. But we stayed in touch, and she wrote me that Barbara gave birth to a little girl."

"But you didn't come back," Jenna stated.

"No." He bowed his head. If he *was* an actor, Jenna was surprised he hadn't made it big in Hollywood. The guy looked really sad.

"How did you find me?"

"Research. The Internet." He gave her a half smile. "Your little brush with the police had one positive consequence: your name got on a database or two."

"I never did drugs, you know, no matter what you read," Jenna declared. "I was just with some people who had them." Now, why had she said that? What did she care if this total stranger thought she was a druggie?

"Perhaps I should leave you two alone so you can have a private reunion," Mr. Jackson said as he started to get out of his chair.

"No!" Jenna cried out. "I mean, that's not necessary. Nice to meet you, Mr. Kelley. Can I please go now, Mr. Jackson?'

The principal's eyes darkened, but Stuart Kelley seemed much more understanding. "I know this must come as a huge shock, Jenna. And this is a difficult time for you, with your mother in rehabilitation."

Wow! He really did know a lot about her, Jenna thought, but she said nothing.

"I can understand if you don't want to have any kind of relationship," he continued. "But would you mind if I contacted the family you're staying with?

Perhaps I could visit you there, if it's okay with you."

Jenna swallowed, trying to lose what felt like a gigantic lump in her throat. She supposed there wasn't any harm in that. And the Devons were smart people. They'd be able to figure out who he was and what he was really up to.

So she shrugged. "Whatever."

This time she didn't bother to ask the principal's permission. She turned and walked out.

The secretary, still smiling, handed her a note that would allow her to show up late to whatever class she was supposed to be in now. But that wasn't where she went. Instead, she walked down a silent hall and went straight into a restroom. She needed time alone to think.

Who *was* this guy? And what did he want from her? He had to be pulling some kind of scam, but why? It wasn't as if he could kidnap her and ransom her for money.

Mr. Jackson claimed there was evidence that this Stuart Kelley really was her father. But why would he come looking for her? So he could claim her and get the welfare allowance the state gave her mother? But it wasn't much money—hardly worth the effort. None of this made any sense at all.

She was almost relieved to hear the bell ring. At least class would be a distraction. She left the restroom and practically collided with Amanda Beeson.

"There you are!" Amanda exclaimed. "I've been looking everywhere for you!"

"What do *you* want?" Jenna asked, knowing her rudeness would have no effect whatsoever on Amanda.

She was right. Amanda practically shoved her back into the restroom. "I have a favor to ask you."

The door to one of the stalls opened, and a girl Jenna vaguely recognized came out. She was Nina something, a friend of Amanda's.

"Hi, Amanda. You're Jenna Kelley, aren't you?"

"Yeah, so what?"

"So nothing. I just didn't know you two were friends." Nina sauntered out of the restroom.

The color drained from Amanda's face. Despite everything she'd just been through, Jenna burst out laughing. Clearly, poor Amanda was devastated at having been caught talking to notorious bad girl

Jenna Kelley.

She almost felt sorry for Amanda—but not quite. "Why would I do *you* a favor?"

Amanda recovered from her shock and faced her squarely. "Do you want me to tell everyone you still sleep with a teddy bear?"

"I'll just call you a liar," Jenna replied.

Amanda grinned meanly. "I have a photo."

Jenna doubted that. When Amanda had been Tracey and they'd slept in the same room, she didn't recall ever seeing a camera. And with everything else on her mind now, and her reputation not exactly squeaky clean, did she really care if people knew she slept with a teddy bear?

But she had to admit—she was curious to know what Amanda could possibly want her to do. "What kind of favor?"

"I want you to read Ken's mind. I've been flirting with him like crazy, and he's totally not responding."

Jenna cocked her head to one side. "Did it ever occur to you that maybe Ken just doesn't want to be with you?"

"No," Amanda replied. "There's got to be another

reason. You have to find out what it is."

It was so annoying—the way Amanda just assumed that every girl wanted to be her friend and every boy was madly in love with her. And there was something else about this that bugged Jenna.

"Weren't you listening when Madame said we shouldn't use one another to exploit our gifts?"

"Since when do you do what the teachers say?" Amanda retorted.

She had a point. But Jenna shook her head. "Look, Amanda, if he's not interested in you, then he's not thinking about you. What difference would it make if I found out that he was thinking about—I don't know—football, or soccer, or macaroni and cheese? How would that help you?"

Amanda was momentarily at a loss for words.

"I've got a better idea," Jenna said. "You're a body snatcher. Why don't you just take over his body? Then you could fall in love with yourself. It shouldn't be too difficult, considering how conceited you are."

And she walked out of the restroom, pleased that for two whole minutes she hadn't thought about the mysterious Mr. Kelley.

# Chapter Seven

A S JENNA LEFT THE restroom, half a dozen girls entered, and several of them greeted Amanda. But she was barely aware of them. She walked out in a daze, with Jenna's words still ringing in her ears. Not the part about being conceited. She didn't care one little bit what Jenna thought of her. It was Jenna's idea that was stuck in her head.

Would it work? Could she really take over Ken's body and make him fall in love with her? Of course, if she was inside Ken, her physical self would be that robotic Other-Amanda who took over when she was elsewhere. But so what? That Amanda-robot-thing acted just like her. And once she-as-Ken asked Other-Amanda out, she'd get back inside herself and charm him on their date. It was just a question of getting him alone, of having his full attention.

There was only one problem—but it was a big one. How could she take over Ken's body? Body snatching worked only when she felt enormous sympathy for someone. How could she ever feel sorry for Ken? He was good-looking, he was popular, and she was pretty sure he had no problems with schoolwork. She didn't know much about his family, but she'd seen them all together at a restaurant recently. Thinking back, she recalled two parents and a little sister. They had seemed okay—a normal, ordinary family.

But maybe his parents weren't getting along— maybe they were even heading for divorce. There'd been no evidence of that when she'd seen them, but you never knew what went on behind the scenes. She'd have to ask her mother—*she* kept up to date on community gossip. Amanda knew it wasn't very kind of her to hope that Ken's parents were breaking up, but at least it would give her something to pity.

Or maybe the whole idea was absolutely stupid. First of all, she didn't have that kind of control over her gift. She could avoid body snatching by not feeling sorry for someone, but could she actually initiate a snatch? She'd never tried because she'd never wanted to, and there was no reason to think she had the ability.

On the other hand, since she'd never tried, she didn't know if she couldn't.

So what if she could make this happen? What if she could take over Ken's body, ask out robot-Amanda, and then get back inside herself just in time for the big date? Would Ken even remember that he'd asked her out?

She thought back to her time inside Tracey's body. She'd never really talked to Tracey about it, so she wasn't sure how much Tracey remembered after she got her body back. But after she'd been inside Tracey for a while, she *had* felt some sort of connection, like Tracey knew what was going on.

So what if Ken did remember and he wasn't happy about what Amanda had made him do? She could make things even worse than they already were.

Not to mention the weirdness of being inside *Ken's* body. It was one thing to act like Tracey Devon; how could she possibly act like a boy? No, it was insane—she could never pull it off. She'd have to come up with something else.

But what? This was so frustrating—it was driving her crazy.

"Hello, hello, is anyone home? Earth to Amanda! Come in, Amanda."

She turned to see Nina, Sophie, and Britney walking alongside her. She had no idea how long they'd been there, but they were all giggling.

"What's so funny?" she demanded.

"You," Nina said. "You look so out of it! Have you been taking lessons from Emily Sanders?"

"Don't be stupid," Amanda snapped. "I've just got something on my mind, that's all. Honestly, can't a person think about something? And don't ask me what I'm thinking about, because it's none of your business!"

Now all three girls were staring at her, and she wanted to kick herself for going all postal like that. Why had she sounded so annoyed? Getting upset like that—it was so uncool.

"Don't bite off our heads!" Nina exclaimed. "I don't know what's happened to you lately, Amanda."

Sophie nodded. "You're just not yourself."

Britney chimed in. "Ever since you got stuck in that weird class, it's like you've changed."

"I have *not!*" she declared indignantly.

The three girls exchanged looks, and Amanda knew immediately that they'd been talking about her behind her back. This was bad.

Her mind began to race. Personally, she didn't think she'd been behaving any differently, but clearly they did, so she had to do something to provide an excuse for her attitude. She needed a problem, but it had to be a cool problem, something that would give her status.

"It's Ken," she said suddenly.

They all looked puzzled. "Ken Preston?" Britney asked.

Amanda nodded. "He likes me. I can tell. He's been coming on to me like crazy—flirting at school, calling me at home, sending me instant messages . . ."

Now her friends looked confused. "What's wrong with that?" Sophie wanted to know. "Ken is *hot.*"

"Oh, sure, I know that," Amanda said carelessly. "I'm just not sure how I feel about him. And I don't want to hurt his feelings."

Uh-oh—wrong comment. The notorious Queen of Mean Amanda Beeson didn't care if she hurt someone's feelings. Was it her imagination or did all three of the girls just take a step backward, creating more of a distance between them? And ohmigod, was that Tracey Devon coming toward them? The old Tracey Devon would never have had the guts to approach Amanda Beeson. She'd created a monster!

"Amanda, hi. I just wanted to tell you that I'm sorry if I embarrassed you in class today. But I really want you to know how grateful I am—"

Amanda grabbed her arm and pulled her away from the others. "Shut up!" she hissed in Tracey's ear. "My friends don't know about me!"

Tracey's eyebrows went up. "Really? But I thought—"

"I have to get to class," Amanda said frantically, turning her back on Tracey. But her friends were already halfway down the hall. She raced to catch up with them.

"Wait up," she demanded.

"Sorry," Nina said. "We wanted to give you some

privacy with your new best friend, Tracey."

Britney started to giggle and then quickly clamped her hand over her mouth. Britney Teller, who worshiped Amanda! Could her life get any worse?

It could. Because here came Ken Preston, ambling down the hall.

"Hi, Ken!" Nina called out, and she stepped aside to reveal Amanda, practically pointing at her. Ken glanced in their direction.

"Hi, Nina."

That was it. Not a word of greeting to Amanda.

"I don't think you're going to have to worry about breaking his heart, Amanda," Nina said. "He didn't even look at you. Oops! The bell's going to ring." Everyone took off in different directions.

This wasn't good. Amanda wasn't just teetering on her pinnacle anymore— she was slipping off. This couldn't be happening to her.

But throughout the rest of the school day, she saw sign after sign of her diminishing popularity. She received no compliments, not even for her new shoes. When she went into her algebra class, she saw that her friends Emma and Katie had their heads together. And when they saw her, they immediately moved apart. She knew what that meant. They'd been talking about her, too.

The worst was yet to come. There was an assembly scheduled that day, during the next-to-last period— another one of those dull programs on the environment. They'd been having them every week—on global warming, recycling, all kinds of boring topics. Amanda had no idea what this week's subject was, and she didn't care—she had bigger things to worry about than the future of the dumb planet.

But everyone liked assemblies, even boring ones. You got out of class, and assemblies were a good excuse to spend time with your friends. You could sit wherever you wanted, so it was like the cafeteria, where the cliques could gather. Best of all, assemblies were usually held in the gym and the students sat on the bleachers. The coolest kids commandeered the highest level, where they could ignore the speakers and talk to one another without being seen by the teachers.

Amanda's gang always sat on the top row of the

left side, farthest from the stage. Automatically, she went down to that end of the gym and started up the stairs. She was more than halfway to the top when she was confronted with a sight more horrifying than—well, than any massacre in any horror movie that Amanda had ever seen.

There they were: Nina, Britney, Sophie, Emma, and Katie—and they hadn't saved a space for her. Instead, they'd allowed Cara Winters and Terri Boyd to join them. And now they were squeezing themselves together even more tightly to let in Heather Todd. Heather Todd! Who, just that very morning, had been thrilled to give Amanda a completely illegal photocopy of Ken's class schedule! How was this possible? This couldn't be happening to her. How could someone's reputation totally collapse in one crummy day?

Now Emma had seen her, and she was nudging the others. They were all looking at her, standing there all alone, with no place to sit. For what would have to be the one and only time in Amanda's life, she wished she were Tracey Devon and could just vanish.

But she was Amanda Beeson, ruler of all that was cool at Meadowbrook Middle School, and if nothing else, she could try to preserve some dignity. Refusing to meet anyone's eyes—but knowing full well that all eyes were on her—she turned and walked down the steps. Now she knew how Marie Antoinette must have felt on her way to the guillotine or how Anne Boleyn had felt when she faced her executioner. Fallen queens, all of them.

By the time she'd reached the bottom, the program was beginning and she had to take the first seat available, at the end of a row of nerdy brainiacs who probably actually *cared* about the environment. At least they weren't paying any attention to her. They didn't even notice her, and for once she was grateful for that.

And unlike Marie Antoinette or Anne Boleyn, she still had a head and she could use it. She would not fall apart. She would deal with this situation and she would overcome it. She would reclaim her throne.

But how? That was the big question. And so she went back to that conversation with Jenna in the restroom and began to consider Jenna's suggestion again.

From her bag, she pulled out the copy of Ken's class schedule. According to it, he had gym class after the assembly. Excellent. This meant that after the last bell, he'd need a few extra minutes to change his clothes. That would give her time to get to that end of the building and position herself somewhere unnoticeable but from where she could see him emerge. Her plan was to follow him home, and just before he arrived, she would corner him.

At that point, she had two options. She could flirt—but that hadn't worked so far. The second possibility was to discover something about him that would elicit her sympathy and, she hoped, give her the means to take over his body. She strongly suspected that this option was the better one. If she could control Ken, she could make him do what she wanted him to do: hang out with Amanda, date Amanda, make the whole school believe that he was madly in love with Amanda, and put her back up on the pedestal where she belonged. And even if it wasn't real, even if he didn't want her once she gave him back his body, so what? She'd already be back on top, and she could let everyone think *she*'d broken up with him, which would give her only more prestige.

Yes, the second option was definitely the one to go with. True, she'd never before tried to take over a body on purpose, but Amanda Beeson always got what she wanted. And if she wanted her life back, she'd figure out a way.

Somehow, she made it through her last class without having to pay too much attention. The second the bell rang, she was out the door, and in minutes she was at the other end of the school building. There was an exit just outside the gym from which Ken would undoubtedly emerge, and she stationed herself around the side of the building. She'd see him come out, he'd pass without seeing her, and she could follow him from a safe distance. Behind her and down a small slope was the playing field, and as she waited, she could hear the soccer team gathering out there for their afterschool practice.

She didn't have to wait long. And she was in luck—he was alone. She plastered herself against the wall to make sure he didn't see her when he passed.

Unfortunately, he didn't go in the direction that she'd anticipated. He turned and walked right past her. But fortunately, he behaved just as he'd been behaving toward her lately. He didn't even see her.

He was watching the soccer practice. His back was to her as he stood on the edge of the slope and gazed out at the boys on the field. She couldn't see his face, but something about his posture made her think that he wasn't in a very good mood.

He'd been the captain of the soccer team, she remembered. Then he'd had some kind of bad accident, and he couldn't play anymore. He probably missed his sport.

She edged along the wall to get into a position where she could have a better look at him. She wasn't any good at reading faces, and she certainly couldn't read his mind, but maybe he'd notice her and be happy to have some company. Once she could see his face, she knew he was feeling something stronger than simple regret.

She'd never seen a boy look so sad before. He must have really loved playing soccer. She could almost swear she saw a tear in his eye, which was ridiculous, of course, because cool guys like Ken didn't cry.

Or did they? Because now she could see the tear trickling down his cheek. Stunned, it took her a moment to react before she scampered out of his line of sight. He'd be so humiliated if a girl saw him crying!

She gave up on her plan to follow him and started toward home. All the way there, that image of Ken kept flashing before her eyes. What was that all about? She'd heard that guys could be seriously devoted to their sports. Her own father loved golf, and if he couldn't play for some reason, he'd probably feel kind of sad. But he wouldn't *cry*. Soccer must have really meant a lot to Ken. He'd looked totally depressed.

No matter how hard she tried, she couldn't get that image of him out of her mind. It was funny, in a way. Seeing a guy looking all demoralized like that certainly wasn't a turn-on. It didn't make Ken very appealing as a potential boyfriend. Some girls might like the sensitive type, but not Amanda. Public displays of emotion, particularly by boys, weren't her thing.

Lying in bed that night, she couldn't sleep. If she had to write off Ken as a possible way to get back her crown, what were her other options? She could make a huge fuss and demand that her parents get her out of that stupid gifted class, but that could also make things worse. It would be like admitting that the gifted class had been a bad place to be, and it would raise only more questions.

She tried to think of other actions she could take, but for some reason, she couldn't concentrate. This was truly bizarre, because she never had a hard time thinking about herself—she was her own favorite subject. But her mind kept going back to Ken and his expression while he watched the soccer practice.

This made no sense to her at all. She'd basically written him off as boyfriend material, so why couldn't she stop thinking about him? As she finally felt sleep begin to descend on her, she knew with despair that she'd end up dreaming about Ken Preston that night.

But as it turned out, she did more than that.

# CHAPTER EIGHT

ARE YOU NERVOUS?" Tracey asked. Sitting on the bed, Jenna pulled her knees up to her chest and wrapped her arms around her legs.

"No."

Tracey grinned. "Liar."

Jenna relented. "Okay, but you have to admit, this is all pretty weird. I'm just about to sit down to have dinner with some complete stranger who claims he's my father. Wouldn't you be nervous?"

"I'd be a wreck," Tracey said. "Something like this could make me disappear again."

"Wish *I* could disappear," Jenna grumbled. But since she couldn't, she went the opposite route. Hopping off the bed, she went back to Tracey's dressing table, sat down, and reapplied her makeup. She added more kohl to her eyes and a thick layer of purple stain to her lips.

"How do I look?" she asked Tracey.

"Like someone I wouldn't want to run into walking alone through a dark alley," Tracey replied.

"Good." That was precisely the image she wanted to convey. Whoever this man was, she wanted to make sure he could see she was a tough chick, not some wimpy little girl who was craving a father figure.

"How come you weren't in class today?" Tracey asked.

"Because I didn't want Madame asking me how I felt about this Stuart Kelley guy showing up. I'm sure Mr. Jackson told her about it."

"How *do* you feel?"

"Tracey!"

"Okay! Sorry."

"Did I miss anything thrilling?"

Tracey shook her head. "Martin gave his career report. He said that with his special gift, he'd like to be a mercenary."

"He wants to be a soldier?"

"Not exactly. He thinks people would pay him to beat up their enemies."

"What about Ken? Maybe he could conduct séances to put people in contact with their dead relatives. That would make Emily happy."

"Ken wasn't there either. Emily said she could be a TV weather reporter, and Charles said he could hire himself out to couch-potato types so they'd never have to get out of their comfy chairs for another bag of chips. Madame suggested that he could help people who were like him, who couldn't get around easily, but he said he thought couch potatoes would pay more."

Jenna grinned. That was very Charles. She was enjoying this conversation—it kept her mind off the upcoming dinner. "How about Amanda? What does she think she could do with her gift?"

"Madame didn't call on her today, which was probably a good thing. She was looking even blanker than usual."

The sound of a doorbell made Jenna stiffen. "Uh-oh! Here he is. Whoever he is."

"You could always read his mind and find out."

Jenna nodded. That was exactly what she planned to do when the right moment came around. She took a deep breath. "Okay, let's go."

The Devon Seven, already fed and bathed, had been banished to their room with their babysitter so that the others could have a real grown-up dinner. When Tracey and Jenna arrived in the living room, they found Mr. Devon fixing cocktails and Mrs. Devon holding a huge bouquet of roses.

"Jenna, look what your father brought us!"

Refusing to smile, Jenna nodded. "They're very pretty."

"Tracey, would you find a vase?"

Jenna gave her friend a fierce don't-leave-me look, but Tracey took the flowers from her mother and went off toward the kitchen.

"Hello, Jenna." The stranger was smiling at her.

"Hi," she murmured.

Now that she'd recovered from the shock she'd felt in Mr. Jackson's office, she could get a good look at this man. He was definitely what Emily had predicted—tall, dark, and handsome. He was dressed neatly in a suit and tie, and he looked perfectly at ease, as if dinner with a long-lost daughter was an ordinary, everyday event.

Tracey returned with the vase of roses, which her mother placed in the center of the dining table. Then she passed around a tray of crackers with squiggles of something on them.

"What do you think of your daughter, Mr. Kelley?" she asked gaily.

"Please, call me Stuart." He looked at Jenna. "I think she's beautiful," he said simply.

The squiggle on the cracker turned out to be cheese, but that wasn't what Jenna choked on. She stared at the man in disbelief. "*What?*"

Mr. Devon laughed jovially. "I'm sure all fathers think their daughters are beautiful. I know I do—all eight of them."

Stuart Kelley nodded, but his eyes were still on Jenna. "And very special."

"Well, these two certainly are," Mrs. Devon said. "You do know about their special gifts, don't you?"

"The school principal did say something about Jenna having deep insights into people."

"I suppose that's one way of looking at it," Mr. Devon said. "*My* daughter can disappear."

"*Dad!*" Tracey interjected. "We're not really

supposed to talk about this."

Her father brushed that aside. "Mr. Kelley—Stuart, I mean—is one of us. A gifted parent."

Stuart shook his head. "Hardly that, considering I've been missing from Jenna's life. I don't know how I'm ever going to make it up to her."

The Devon parents looked at each other. "We understand," they said in unison.

The way he was looking at her with that adoring expression was getting on Jenna's nerves. "Why did you come looking for me now?" she demanded.

He sighed and took a small sip of his cocktail. Jenna noticed that he'd barely touched it. At least he wasn't an alcoholic—that was something.

"I've been a coward," he said. "I always wanted to see you. I wanted to see your mother, too, but I assumed she'd slam the door in my face. She certainly has the right to do that. I treated her terribly."

"You sure did," Jenna blurted out. "You walked out on her when she was pregnant. No wonder she started drinking."

"Jenna," Mrs. Devon chided her gently, "people make all kinds of mistakes in their lives. At least your father is trying to make amends now."

It dawned on Jenna that they were all talking as if it was an absolute certainty that Stuart Kelley was her real father. Including herself—she'd just accused this man she'd never seen before in her life of walking out on her mother. Maybe now was the time to do a little mental exploration and try to find out who this guy really was.

But Mrs. Devon chose that moment to call them all to the table, and there was no opportunity for Jenna to stare at him and concentrate. The next few moments were taken up with accepting portions of roast beef and scooping green beans onto plates.

Jenna might not have been able to read his mind at the moment, but she hadn't finished asking questions. "Why did you just show up at the door on Monday? Why didn't you call first?"

"I couldn't find a telephone number," he replied.

That was a good point. The phone had been disconnected ages ago because the bill hadn't been paid.

"Besides," he continued, "I assumed your mother would just hang up once she knew who was calling."

"And she would have slammed the door in your face if she'd been home," Jenna countered.

"True," he admitted. "She certainly had every reason to. I just thought I'd have a better chance of talking to her if I came in person."

He probably thought he was so good-looking that she couldn't resist him, Jenna thought sourly. Unfortunately, he was probably right. He was exactly the type of guy her mother liked.

"Have you spoken to her at all?" Mrs. Devon asked.

"No. She's not allowed visitors or phone calls at the hospital. When does she come out, Jenna?"

"A week from Sunday."

"I'm very anxious to see her."

"Why?" Jenna asked bluntly.

He had a dazzling smile. "This might be hard to believe, Jenna, but I was very much in love with your mother. Even when I left her."

Tracey gazed at him curiously. "Do you think you might still be? In love with her, I mean?"

"Tracey!" Jenna glared at her. "Isn't that a little personal?"

Stuart Kelley laughed gently. "It's all right, Jenna. And who knows? All I can say is that I've never stopped thinking about her. And you, Jenna."

Jenna didn't say anything. A new thought had come to her. This man was planning to stick around and see her mother when she came out of rehab. Barbara Kelley might have a foggy memory after all those years of drinking, but she wasn't stupid. Surely she'd know her own ex-husband.

Jenna looked at him now and tried to imagine him as her father. Maybe . . . *maybe* this wasn't quite as far-fetched as it seemed. An image flashed across her mind: a family, made up of a mother and a father and a daughter, living in a real house, having a normal life . . .

With effort, she pushed the picture out of her head. She was not optimistic by nature, and she wasn't going to start looking on the bright side of everything now.

There was an uncomfortable silence at the table. Stuart Kelley must have felt it, because he changed the subject. "So your father said you can disappear, Tracey?"

Jenna almost smiled. She liked the way he had said it conversationally, the way someone might say, *So your father said you play the piano?* He wasn't acting like they were freaks, the way some people would have.

"I used to," Tracey said. She looked at her parents, both of whom suddenly became terribly interested in what still lay on their plates. Jenna couldn't blame them—they must have felt awful about how they'd treated their daughter. Tracey was nice enough not to go into the whole story for Stuart.

"I'm practicing now," she went on. "What I need is to be able to *feel* invisible, and it's not so easy for me anymore. But I'm doing these meditation exercises, and they're helping." She turned to Jenna. "Right?"

Jenna agreed. "You were practically translucent last night. I could see the glow from the lamp behind you."

Tracey nodded happily. "We're in a special class, Jenna and me," she told Stuart. "And we're learning how to get in touch with our gifts and control them. Use them wisely."

Stuart turned to Jenna. "Is that working for you, too?"

Jenna shrugged. "Yeah, I guess."

Mr. Devon was looking at her with interest. "How deeply can you read minds, Jenna?"

She shrugged again. "I don't know."

"I mean, can you go beneath the surface?" he continued. "Or can you just read what people are clearly thinking?" He turned to his wife. "Just think of the benefit to therapy. People wouldn't have to be analyzed for years to find out what's going on in their subconscious minds. Jenna could tell them!"

"Let's try it right now," Mrs. Devon said excitedly. She turned to Stuart and explained, "I've been in analysis for years, and we just had a breakthrough last week—an event that I'd buried in my subconscious. Let's see if Jenna can tell me what it was!"

"Mom!" Tracey moaned. "Don't ask Jenna to do that—it's embarrassing!"

Jenna could feel her face turning red. She *was* embarrassed, but how could she say no to the woman who was providing her with a home at the moment?

Tracey hadn't finished. "Besides, Madame says we should never exploit one another's gifts, and that includes the *parents* of the gifted."

"Who is Madame?" Stuart asked.

"Our gifted-class teacher," Jenna told him. "She says we have to be very careful about revealing our gifts. She tells us there are plenty of bad people out there who might want to use us for their own nasty purposes."

"And she's absolutely right," Stuart said firmly. "I don't know what kind of benefit people could get from using your mind-reading skills, but I'm sure they'd think of something." Turning to Tracey, he said, "And someone might try to force you to rob a bank for them. I think it's best not to let too many people know what you can do."

"I agree," Mr. Devon said. "Just keep it in the family."

"That's right." Stuart looked at Jenna. "Keep it in the family," he repeated.

Jenna suddenly became aware of a rush of feeling filling her up. Was this happening? Could this be real?

"You're absolutely right," Mrs. Devon declared. "In fact, I'm ashamed of myself for asking you to show off your gift, Jenna."

"That's okay," Jenna mumbled.

Mrs. Devon raised her wineglass. "Let's toast our gifted daughters and vow never to take advantage of their gifts."

Stuart raised his glass, and so did Mr. Devon. "To our daughters," they intoned.

Tracey looked at Jenna, but Jenna averted her eyes. She suspected that Tracey knew exactly what she was thinking, despite not having any mind-reading skills.

Which reminded her of what she'd planned to do to Stuart Kelley. When Mrs. Devon went into the kitchen to get the dessert, Tracey left to help her, and the two men began talking about some movie they'd both seen. It was a good moment to try a little mind reading.

Since the men were talking, their topic of conversation would probably be the uppermost thing on Stuart's mind. But this would be a good opportunity to try what Mrs. Devon had suggested—to see if she could get below the surface thoughts to something deeper.

Her father's—she corrected herself—*Stuart*'s back was to her, so she had no problem staring. First, she blocked out their voices, the music coming from the stereo, the sounds from the kitchen. Then she concentrated on piercing Stuart's mind.

But she couldn't. She tried again and again, but she couldn't even pick up the superficial thoughts about the movie they were discussing. Was he able to block her, like Emily? No, it was probably Emily's own weird gift that made her unable to be read. This was more like what happened when she tried to read her mother's mind. The family thing . . .

She caught her breath. Then she started coughing.

Mr. Devon poured her some water while Stuart patted her on the back. "Take deep breaths," he ordered. She did, and when the coughs died down, she drank the water.

"Are you okay?" Stuart asked.

"I'm fine," she assured her father. And in her mind, she added, *Maybe more than fine.*

# CHAPTER NINE

AMANDA HAD NOW HAD 24 hours to practice being a boy. Well, not exactly *being* a boy—other than using the toilet, she hadn't really done anything boyish. But she'd had a day to get used to *feeling* like a boy. Which wasn't long. So she still felt very, very strange.

When she'd realized, the morning before, that she was now inside Ken Preston's body, she'd been pretty stunned. Even though that had been one of her original plans, she hadn't been aware that she'd been feeling sorry for Ken. But apparently those feelings she'd had after seeing him on Tuesday were real sympathy and pity, not simply distaste at seeing a boy cry.

So now she was in a body unlike any she'd ever known before. Thinking about it now, she *had* been a boy once—little Martin Cooper from the gifted class, years ago when he'd lived across the street from her and she'd seen him being bullied. But that had lasted only a minute or two, and at that age, she probably hadn't been all that aware of the difference between boys and girls anyway.

Now she was very much aware. When she'd climbed out of bed the day before, she couldn't even bring herself to take off her clothes to have a shower—it had been just too embarrassing to look at the body she was in. She'd realized that, other than babies and statues, she'd never seen a totally nude male before. It was all too much. So when Ken's mother appeared at the door and demanded to know why he hadn't come down for breakfast, she pretended to have an upset stomach and a sore throat. For a moment, Amanda was afraid that Mrs. Preston might call a doctor, but instead she decided he should stay in bed and see how he felt the next day. Then Mrs. Preston took Ken's little sister to school. And as it turned out, she had a job, so Amanda could be alone and had the house to herself all day.

With this body, so different from her own,

nothing was easy. Talking, moving, eating—everything felt as though she were in a costume. Walking on legs that weren't her own was particularly difficult—she kept stumbling and tripping as she moved around Ken's house. When she spoke out loud and heard someone else's voice, it utterly freaked her out.

Of course, she'd had the experience of spending a long time inside another person's body, but at least Tracey Devon was a girl. And something interesting occurred to her. Despite the fact that Tracey was a total nerd and she, Amanda, was fabulous, it hadn't been this hard being Tracey. She shuddered to think that maybe she and Tracey had more in common than she'd ever suspected.

Size made a big difference. She and Tracey were approximately the same height, but Ken was a lot taller. Going up and down stairs, reaching for things— everything like that felt awkward. There was no way she'd go back to school until she could feel—well, not normal (she couldn't hope for that), but at least not goofy.

She still felt goofy that morning, but she couldn't stay at home another day or Ken's mother would drag her to a doctor. So she got up, showered with her eyes closed, put on jeans and a T-shirt, and just hoped that Ken wouldn't have to wear a tie while she was in his body—she had no idea how guys made those knots.

Checking herself out in the mirror, she wasn't displeased. If she had to be a boy, at least she was a good-looking one. And she had to admit it was kind of nice not to have to spend the usual time fixing her hair and putting on makeup.

She went down to the kitchen. Ken's father had already left for work, and his mother was helping his little sister with her coat.

"Feeling better?" she asked Ken–Amanda.

"Yeah, fine," she replied. She took a bowl and examined the cereal boxes on the counter. "Don't we have any Special K?"

Mrs. Preston was taken aback. "Special K? Why would we have that?"

Amanda always ate Special K in the morning, because it was supposed to be good for her figure. How stupid of her—guys probably didn't worry about stuff like that. She'd have to be more careful about what she said.

"Oh, I was just curious what it tastes like," she lied.

Mrs. Preston still looked puzzled. "You've been eating Cocoa Puffs since you've had teeth, Ken. I can't believe you're interested in trying something else now."

"I'm a teenager," Amanda said lamely. "We do crazy things." She poured herself some Cocoa Puffs and was amazed to find how good they were. It occurred to her that boys always seemed to eat a lot more than girls. She'd have to take advantage of this body and indulge in the treats she was always denying her real self.

Luckily, she could remember Ken's schedule from constantly looking at that photocopy she had, so she knew where to go when she arrived at school. Unfortunately, she didn't know his locker number, so she'd have to lug his stuff around with her all day, but Ken used a backpack, so that wasn't too bad.

She'd just walked into his homeroom when she felt a hard smack on her shoulders. "Hey!" she cried out in outrage, before she remembered that guys were always slapping one another on the back.

Barry Levin looked at him in surprise. "What's the matter?"

"Oh, nothing—I, um, pulled a muscle," she said

quickly. "What's up?"

"Not much. You ready for the French test?"

Her heart sank. Amanda took Spanish. "Nah, I'm toast. I'm gonna blow it."

Barry grinned. "Yeah, right. Mister Straight A is gonna blow a test."

She managed a sickly smile. With any luck, there would be a smart person sitting in front of her whose paper she could copy.

As the day went on, she discovered some interesting facts about the social life of boys. They didn't gossip about one another, they didn't compliment one another's clothes or hair, they didn't talk behind one another's backs. She didn't have to talk much at all—she just acted interested in whatever sport the other guys were discussing. Fortunately, Ken had a reputation for being pretty quiet, so nobody seemed to expect him to take the lead in conversations.

Her one slip-up came when some guy at lunch announced he'd seen a mouse run across the cafeteria floor.

"Ew, gross!" she shrieked. The other boys stared at her.

She managed a feeble grin. "I'm just making up for the fact that we don't have any chicks at the table."

It wasn't a very good excuse, and the boys still looked perplexed, but within seconds they were talking about something else and seemed to have forgotten her outburst. Which was another thing she decided was different about boys—if a girl did something uncool, her friends never let her forget it. At least, that's the way it was with *her* friends.

By the time lunch was over, she was feeling pretty satisfied with the way she'd pulled off her Ken behavior with his friends. No one was acting strangely around her or staring at her. Getting along as a boy with other boys wouldn't be all that difficult, she decided.

But getting along with girls might be. She was on her way out of the cafeteria when Cara Winters cornered her.

"Hi, Ken," she said coyly. "Are you feeling okay?"

"Sure. Why wouldn't I be?"

"You were out yesterday."

"Oh, yeah. No big deal—just didn't feel like going

to school."

Cara looked surprised, and Amanda realized that Ken was not the type to cut classes whenever he was in that sort of mood.

She amended her remark. "I had a sore throat. But I'm fine now."

"Oh, good. I was just wondering . . . could we get together before French today and go over some conjugations?"

So Cara was in the French class. "Uh, well, I haven't really studied."

Now she looked really surprised. "You haven't?"

"I completely forgot we were having the test today, and then I wasn't feeling good, so . . ." She let Ken's voice trail off, and Cara nodded understandingly. She moved in closer.

"I'll arrange the paper on my desk so you can see my answers," she whispered. "Of course, I know you don't like to cheat, but . . ."

"Maybe I could make an exception this time," Amanda replied.

Cara looked positively thrilled. And Amanda remembered a time when *she*'d been flattered that a guy had wanted to copy her paper. Boys really had it made.

Of course, her real test would come in the gifted class. Could she pull off her Ken act there? Last month, when she was Tracey, Madame could tell something was up after only a few days. And now she'd be sitting in the same room with her robotic other self. Would anyone sense that something was just slightly off?

She timed her entrance just like Ken did, at the last minute. And so did Other-Amanda. They practically collided at the door of room 209.

"Hi, Ken."

Could there be anything stranger than hearing your own voice speaking to you? Yes—seeing yourself through someone else's eyes. She couldn't even bring herself to look.

"Hi," she mumbled, just like Ken would have, and hurried into the room. Taking Ken's seat, she let Ken's silky blond hair fall into his eyes and peered out in a way that she hoped was unobtrusive.

Madame rose from her desk. "Yesterday we were talking about the ways in which you might be able to use your gift in your chosen career. Martin had just finished telling us that he wanted to hire himself out to people who wanted an enemy to be hurt. Does anyone have a question to ask him?"

Emily raised her hand. "Martin, you have to get really angry at someone before your super strength comes out. How are you going to get angry at the people you're hired to beat up if you don't have any personal connection to them?"

Amanda wasn't particularly interested in Martin's reply, which she knew would be long and rambling. She tuned him out and spent the time looking surreptitiously at herself.

She knew some girls who actually believed they were prettier than they really were. She was not one of them. Last month she'd seen herself through Tracey's eyes, and she knew she was extremely cute. Now she looked even better. She wasn't sure if it was her last haircut or the fact that she was looking through a boy's eyes, but she was even more impressed with herself. What she couldn't understand was why Ken wasn't more interested . . .

*Ken . . .*

The voice seemed to come out of nowhere. Literally. Madame was giving Martin a long, stern lecture on nonviolence, and no one else in the class was speaking.

*Ken?*

It was in her head, she realized. The voice was coming from deep inside. She wasn't hearing it in the ordinary way, through her ears. It was something else.

*Are you there? Can you hear me? It's Rick.*

And suddenly, she understood. It was one of Ken's dead people, trying to communicate.

She didn't know whether to be intrigued or annoyed. On the one hand, the voice wasn't frightening at all. It was young and male and pleasant. On the other hand, she realized that *this* was why Ken always seemed so distracted.

She wasn't sure if she could talk back to the voice, but she tried. In her mind, she thought, *What do you want?*

*Nothing special. Just wanted to talk.*

She replied, *I don't want to talk. Go away.*

There was a moment of silence, and then the

voice, softer this time, said, *Okay*. And her head was silent.

She couldn't believe it. It was so easy! All Ken had to do was tell the voices to go away, and they would obey! At least, this one did. It occurred to her that while she was inside Ken's body, she could do more than just ask herself out. She could lose Ken's gift for him! Then the two of them could unite, confront Madame, and drop out of the class together. And even if he wasn't madly in love with Amanda, he'd be eternally grateful, they could act like a couple, she'd be back on top—everything was falling into place.

And she'd be helping Ken, just like she'd helped Tracey. Not that helping other people was a high priority for her, but she had to admit (only to herself and never to anyone else) that it gave her kind of a nice feeling.

The discussion of Martin's aggressive instincts took up the whole class session, which was fine with Amanda. Madame never called on Ken or Other-Amanda, and the other students had no problem picking on Martin for 50 minutes. Amanda was beginning to understand why the little guy was an eternal victim.

She'd planned to approach herself as soon as class was over, but Other-Amanda took off the second the bell rang. It didn't really matter—she needed more time to prepare what she was going to say, and there wasn't much time between classes for a conversation. She'd meet up with Other-Amanda at her own locker after the last class.

Ken's next class was French, and even though she'd never cheated on a test before, she didn't feel the least bit guilty copying the answers from Cara. She reasoned that she wasn't really Ken or herself either, so the rules didn't count. The only problem would be if Ken got caught—but he didn't.

She got through the rest of the day without any real problems—she just never raised her hand and none of the teachers called on Ken. The only class she now had to worry about was the last one—gym. If she didn't perform well, she could blame it on having been sick the day before, but changing in and out of the gym outfit could be tricky, especially surrounded by all those boys.

But once again, she lucked out. Ken's gym class was

having a lecture day on nutrition. She could sit in the back of a normal classroom and zone out.

She used the time to revise her original plan. She'd meet Amanda at her locker and set up some kind of date for after school that day or the next. Saturday at the latest. Once they were alone together, she'd take back her own body and let him have his. How she was going to do this, she wasn't quite sure, but she'd worry about that when the time came. Then she'd tell him how she'd lost the voices for him, he'd be grateful, and everything would fall into place.

*Ken?*

There he was again, the dead guy. *Get lost*, she said.

*Ken, what's the matter with you? Why are you acting like this?*

*Because I'm not in the mood*, she responded. *I might never be in the mood again.*

*Please, Ken. Don't say that. I don't know what I'd do without you.*

Despite herself and all her intentions, the voice touched her. The guy sounded so sad. Maybe it wouldn't hurt to have just one real conversation with one of Ken's dead people. She'd have a better understanding of what his gift was really like.

*What do you want?* she asked.

*I'm feeling really down. I can't stop thinking about her.*

*Who?*

*You know! Nancy.*

Amanda didn't know anyone named Nancy. It was kind of an old-fashioned name, she thought. A grandmother-type name. Apparently, this guy—what did he say his name was? Rick—apparently, Rick had talked about this Nancy to Ken before.

*Why are you thinking about Nancy?*

*I'm always thinking about her—you know that. I miss her so much. Like I said, I really loved her. I still can't believe she dumped me at the senior prom.*

*And you couldn't get her back?*

*How could I? That was the night I died.*

This was getting interesting. So she was talking to someone who had to have been around 17 or 18 years old when he died. She wondered how that had happened. She couldn't ask—Ken probably knew.

*Do you know what it feels like, Ken?*

*To die?*

*No, to love someone so much. And to have your*

*heart broken.*

*No, not really.*

*You're lucky. It's the most unbelievable pain. You'd rather have two broken legs than a broken heart. She was everything to me: the sun, the moon, the stars. I can remember thinking I would die for her. Which is ironic, in a way. I did die, but I didn't even have the satisfaction of doing it for her.*

"Ken?"

He looked up. The room was empty, and the teacher was standing at the door.

"Class is over, Ken. I see you didn't find the topic of essential daily vitamins very exciting. But you could have tried to stay awake, just out of common courtesy." The teacher didn't wait for an apology.

Amanda got up, slung Ken's backpack over his shoulder, and hurried out. There were just a few stragglers left in the hall, heading to the exit.

She knew her own habits. Other-Amanda would be long gone. She'd been so caught up in Rick's story that she'd missed her chance to ask herself out.

It looked like she was going to have to be Ken for a while longer.

# CHAPTER TEN

ENNA WAS AT HER LOCKER on Friday afternoon when Tracey joined her.

"Ready to leave?" Tracey asked.

Jenna took out her jacket. "I'm not going home, remember? I'm meeting my father."

"Oh, right." Tracey smiled. "Did you hear what you just said? *My father.*"

Jenna grinned. "Yeah. And it felt so natural."

"You don't have any more doubts?"

Jenna shook her head. "It's like I told you—I couldn't read his mind, just like I can't read my mother's. We're family."

Tracey looked thoughtful. "But you can't read Madame's mind, or Emily's, and they're not family."

"That's different. Emily does something with her own gift, so I can't use mine on her. And Madame . . . she's got some weird insight. Did you notice how she was looking at Amanda today in class?"

"Yeah. What was that all about?"

"Maybe that wasn't the real Amanda."

"She seemed real enough to me," Tracey said.

Jenna slammed the locker door shut. "Yeah, and she seemed real last month, too, when she was actually occupying your body. I'll bet she's inside someone else right now."

"Who?"

"Who knows?" The girls walked to the exit together. "Who cares? But if she wasn't there, I'll bet Madame could tell."

"Could *you* tell? If you read her mind?"

Jenna shrugged. "I guess I could. But like I said, who cares?" They were outside now. "I'm meeting my father at the mall. I'll see you tonight."

As she crossed the street to reach the mall, she could feel the excitement rising inside her. She was meeting her father! It was almost too much to take in. And she wasn't just excited—she was nervous. This would be their first time alone together. Not really alone, of course—there were plenty of other people milling around the mall. But they'd have only each other to talk to. What if she couldn't think of anything to say? What if she bored him? A couple of hours alone with her and he just might decide this relationship wasn't worth the effort.

And what if he wasn't there? What if her original doubts had been on target? What if—

What if he was right there, in front of the music store, where he'd said he'd be, waiting for her?

Mentally kicking herself for having doubts, she waved to him, and he waved back.

"How was your day?" he asked.

"Fine," she replied automatically. "How was yours?"

"Fine," he said. There was a silence.

"It's not easy, is it?" he said. "You'd think that with all these years to catch up on, we wouldn't have any problem coming up with subjects for conversation."

She smiled awkwardly. She wasn't exactly ready to pour out all her feelings and experiences—not yet. She needed something not too personal to get this relationship off the ground.

She glanced at the display in the store window. "What kind of music do you like?"

"A little bit of almost everything," he replied. "Classical, jazz, rock. I'm not too crazy about folk music."

Jenna lit up. "I *hate* folk music! Do you like techno?"

"I can't say I know much about it," he admitted. "Want to introduce me?"

They went into the music store, and Jenna showed him CDs of the groups she particularly liked. There were headphones hanging on the walls so that you could listen to samples, and she showed him how to use them.

He was *cool*. He didn't pull that fake adult thing of pretending to love all the music she played for him, just to prove that he was down with the younger generation. He liked some groups, he didn't like others, and he expressed his opinions openly.

"I think I could get into this," he told her. "I'm going to write down some names so I can download them to my iPod."

She was impressed. "You have an iPod?"

"Absolutely. When you move around as much as I've been moving these past few years, it's the only way to keep your music with you. Don't you have one?"

She shook her head.

"I thought all kids had iPods."

She picked up a CD at random and pretended to study the track listing. "They're pretty expensive," she said finally.

He was silent, and she looked up.

"It's been hard on you and your mother, hasn't it?" he asked. "Financially, I mean."

Jenna shrugged. "We manage."

"Do you?"

She looked away, and he got the message.

"I could say I'm sorry," he said. "I *am* sorry. But there wasn't much I could have done about that. I haven't been doing too well myself. Still, that's no excuse."

Jenna thought it was, and she wanted to make him feel better. "If you didn't have any money, you couldn't have sent us any."

He smiled. "You're a pragmatist. Just like your mother."

"What's a pragmatist?"

"Someone who's down-to-earth, sensible."

Jenna would never have used those words to describe her mother. But maybe Barbara Kelley had been different back when Stuart had known her.

"But I can afford to buy my daughter an iPod," he said suddenly. "Do they sell them here?"

"You don't have to do that," she said.

"I want to," he insisted.

But she had meant what she'd said. The thought of him suddenly showering her with gifts . . . It bothered her.

And to her utter amazement and delight, he understood. "You think I'm trying to buy your affection, don't you?"

She nodded.

He smiled sadly. "You're probably right. Well, you'll let me buy you a Coke, won't you?"

She could agree to that. They went into a café, and she allowed him to buy her not only a Coke but also a plate of fries to share with him. She was a little worried that he was going to start pressing her for information about herself, that he'd expect her to tell him her life story. But once again, he was cool.

He told her about his life, the adventures he'd had.

He'd been living pretty much hand to mouth for the past 13 years, but he'd been doing it in interesting ways. He'd been a porter on a train that went across the country, from New York to San Francisco. He'd washed dishes on a cruise ship. He'd been a waiter in a fancy Hollywood restaurant, and he'd seen lots of famous people in person. He'd worked on a pipeline in Alaska.

He was amazing. Other kids she knew, their fathers were lawyers, teachers, salesmen. They worked in offices, factories, ugly high rises. Tracey's father had some kind of big-and-boring business. None of them were like Stuart Kelley.

And he was better looking than any father she'd ever seen. Tracey's father was practically bald. Emily's dad had a stomach that hung over his belt. Stuart Kelley could be a movie star! Jenna hadn't missed the looks he got from women they'd passed in the mall.

Like the cashier at the café. She took the bill that Stuart gave her without looking at it. She couldn't take her eyes off his face.

"I hope you enjoyed your meal, sir," she gushed.

Stuart kept a perfectly straight face as he said, "It

was an absolutely delicious Coca-Cola."

He was *funny*, Jenna thought in delight. The cashier didn't get it. She just simpered as she handed him some coins.

"Excuse me," Stuart said, looking at the change in his hand. "I think you've made a mistake. I gave you a twenty-dollar bill."

"Oh no, sir, it was a ten," the cashier said.

Stuart looked at her doubtfully. "Are you sure? I'm positive it was a twenty."

Jenna couldn't resist. She focused on the cashier and read her mind.

*This is the easiest ten bucks I've ever made.*

"It was a twenty," Jenna announced.

The cashier pressed her lips together tightly. A man in a white shirt with a tag that read *Manager* came over.

"Is there a problem?" he asked.

"No problem," the cashier said and took a ten-dollar bill from the drawer. "Here's your change, sir."

"Thank you," Stuart said politely.

"Did you see me give her the money?" he asked Jenna as they went back out into the mall.

"No. But I read her mind and I could see that she was trying to cheat you."

He laughed. "That's quite a talent you have, Jenna. I guess I won't have to worry about anyone trying to cheat *you*. Or me, while I've got you around! I think we'd better stick together. What do you think?"

"Sounds okay to me," Jenna said lightly, but she knew her smile was extending from ear to ear.

From there, they did some window-shopping, exchanging comments on fashion, books, art. Stuart had to pick up a few things at the drugstore, and they discovered they both used the same brand of toothpaste.

At one point they paused in front of a tattoo parlor, and Jenna admired the designs displayed in the window.

"Do you like tattoos?" Stuart asked.

She nodded. "I'd like to get one." She watched him carefully to gauge his reaction. Most parents she knew would go ballistic if their kids mentioned getting a tattoo.

Not Stuart. "You might want to wait a while," he said mildly. "Keep in mind that it's pretty much a permanent decision. I know they have treatments to remove them, but that's a big deal and very expensive. I thought about getting one once, a long time ago."

"What kind?" she asked.

"Nothing very original. A name in a heart." He smiled. "*Barbara*."

"I suppose you must be glad you didn't," Jenna remarked, "considering how things worked out."

"Mmm." He smiled wistfully. "Well, you never know. I still might end up with one sometime."

Just any tattoo? Jenna wondered. Or Barbara, in a heart? But she didn't dare ask him. It was too much to hope for.

"Look," he said, "they sell temporary ones. Let's check them out."

They went inside and looked at the various types of press-on tattoos available. Jenna admired a sheet composed of letters and various borders.

"This is cool—you can design your own," she said. "And it says they last at least a week. You could try something, and after a week, if you still like it, you could get a real one tattooed over it."

"Good idea," Stuart agreed. He picked up a sheet and took it to the checkout counter. As they waited in line, he whispered to Jenna, "Keep an eye on the exchange. I don't want you to have to waste your mind-reading skills on me again!"

She grinned. Personally, she didn't think there were any gifts that would be wasted on him.

After paying for the temporary tattoos, Stuart was out of cash, so when they came to a bank, he stopped to get money out of an ATM. There was a woman in front of them, and she was taking an unusually long time. She kept putting in her card, punching numbers, and then taking out the card. Jenna heard her utter a mild curse under her breath.

She turned to them. "I'm sorry I'm taking so long. I can't remember my PIN."

Jenna listened with interest. Here it was—an opportunity to try that subconscious mind reading Mrs. Devon had asked her about. Like an invisible power drill, she bore into the woman's mind.

"Three eight seven two," she said.

The woman stared at her, and her mouth fell open. Then her expression changed to horror.

She jammed the card back into her wallet and took off in a hurry.

"That wasn't very nice of her," Stuart commented.

Jenna laughed. "She must have thought we were thieves."

Stuart started laughing, too. "I guess we make a good team, huh?"

Jenna's heart was so full that she felt like it was going to explode.

It was time for her to get back to the Devons' house. Stuart had a rental car, a cute little yellow compact, and he drove her. Parking in front, he walked her to the door.

"I'm not going to come in," he told her. "It's too close to dinnertime and it'll look like I'm scrounging for a free meal."

Jenna wanted him to stay, but she understood. He was proud, just like her.

"Well, I'll see you," she said. "You're staying in town for a while, aren't you?"

"Absolutely," he assured her. He put his hands on her shoulders, leaned forward, and kissed her lightly on the cheek. Then he pulled back and looked a little embarrassed.

"I hope I wasn't being too pushy there."

Jenna shook her head happily. "No, it's okay. I mean, I guess that's what fathers do, right?"

He smiled. "Right."

# CHAPTER ELEVEN

AMANDA-KEN LAY ON KEN'S bed, staring at the ceiling, and listened. *We spent a lot of time at the beach. The sun on her blond hair—it was like gold sprinkled on gold. Her tan was golden, too. She was like that girl dipped in gold. Did you ever see* Goldfinger?

*No, but I've heard of it. It's an old James Bond movie, right?*

She thought Rick was laughing. *I keep forgetting you're living in another century! I was fourteen when I saw* Goldfinger. *That's how old you are, right? You should see it; it's great.*

*I'll borrow it from the DVD store.*

*Man, I wish we'd had DVDs in my time. That must be so neat, to watch movies whenever you want.*

*Yeah, it's . . . neat.*

*Nancy and I used to go to the movies practically every*

*Saturday night. She liked romantic films, and I liked action ones. Every Saturday, we'd argue about what to see. Not argue, really—more like debate.*

*Who won?*

*We took turns choosing. But she could have won all the time. I'd always give in to her.*

By now, Amanda had figured out how to keep some thoughts to herself. So she could think about how wonderful it would be to have a boyfriend like Rick, who would cherish you and give you anything you wanted. And she didn't have to worry that he might hear that, because Rick still thought he was talking to another guy.

She communicated her next question.

*What else did you guys do together?*

*You know the Public Gardens, near City Hall?*

*Sure.*

*That was one of her favorite places, especially when the roses were in bloom. She loved roses. When I sold my motorcycle, I used the money to give her one red rose every day till the money ran out.*

Red roses and motorcycles. Wow! What a guy.

*What?*

She realized she hadn't kept that thought to herself.

*Um, I was just wondering, why did you sell your motorcycle?*

*My brother joined the army and gave me his to use.* There was a pause. *I don't want to talk about that, okay?*

She wondered if his brother had been killed. Had there been a war going on when Rick was a teenager? She still wasn't sure when that had been.

There was a knock on Ken's bedroom door.

"Come in," Amanda called.

Ken's mother stuck her head in. "Are you feeling all right?"

"Sure. Why?"

"It's Saturday afternoon, the sun's out, and you've been lying in bed all day!" She frowned. "I'm going to call a doctor. You haven't been eating much lately either. I think you need a checkup."

Amanda-Ken jumped off the bed. "I'm fine. I was just thinking about stuff. I'm going out now."

To Rick, she said, *Later.*

What she wanted to do now would require the computer, but she needed to get out of the house before she raised more suspicions in Ken's mother's mind. A teacher had told her class once that there were free online services at the public library. She'd never set foot in the public library before, but she knew where it was.

She was surprised when the librarian at the desk greeted her—greeted Ken, actually.

"Good to see you, Ken," she said with a smile.

Amanda noticed the nameplate on the desk. "Hello, Ms. Fletcher."

The woman looked startled. Then she saw that Ken was staring at the plate, and she turned it around. She laughed softly. "Very funny, Ken. Okay, I just came on and I haven't gotten around to changing the name." She put the plate in a drawer and took out another one that read *Ms. Greenwood.*

Amanda smiled back at the librarian and inwardly breathed a sigh of relief. That was a close call.

Locating the computers, she sat down at one and turned it on. The screen lit up, and then a message appeared.

*Enter Code.*

She got up and went back to the librarian's desk. "The computer says I need a code to log on."

"That's right," she said with a puzzled expression. "Ken, you've used these computers before. You know what to do."

Amanda swallowed. "I, uh, forgot it."

The lines of puzzlement on the librarian's forehead deepened. But at least she answered him. "It's five zeros, Ken. Pretty easy to remember."

"Yeah, right. Of course. I'm a little out of it today."

Now the librarian looked concerned. With Amanda's luck, the woman would turn out to be a friend of Ken's mother and call her to report that Ken was behaving strangely.

Back at the computer, Amanda logged in, and in the search box she typed *Goldfinger*. What came up was a description of the movie, some pictures of the actors, and a date: 1964. How old had Rick said he'd been when he saw it? Fourteen?

She didn't want to go back to Ms. Greenwood or Fletcher or whatever her name was and make a fool of herself again. So she got up and wandered around the library.

It was kind of interesting—she didn't know

libraries had CDs and DVDs and video games. But she didn't take time to look at any of them. She was on a mission.

Finally, she found what she was searching for in a little room off the main area, a room that looked like it hadn't been dusted in years. On a row of shelves she found all the yearbooks of all the schools in town, going back to the dark ages or whatever. If Rick had been 14 in 1964, that meant he probably was supposed to have graduated from high school in 1967 or 1968.

There were three high schools in town. She didn't know his last name. And Rick, or Richard, turned out to be a pretty common name. Checking indexes, she found seven possible Ricks.

She started checking pictures, although she had no idea what she was looking for. In their conversations, there had been no reference to his hair color or any other identifiable characteristic.

It was extremely frustrating. Several of the Ricks looked cute, others not so much. Some of them had really long hair, which must have been the fashion at the time.

There were photos of student activities, teams, and clubs, but she didn't know what Rick had been into in high school. Except Nancy, of course. Which was why she got very excited when she accidentally hit on a picture of a boy and a girl in formal clothes with a caption that read *Rick Lasky and Nancy Chiswick.*

There was always the possibility that there had been another couple named Rick and Nancy. Even so, this felt right. She remembered Rick talking about Nancy's golden hair. This photo was in black and white, but she could see that the girl's long, straight hair was very blond.

She was more interested in the boy. He had straight hair, too, but it looked like a deep brown in the picture. It was almost as long as Nancy's—you never saw hair that long on boys nowadays, except maybe on some hippie-type rock stars. He was thin, but he didn't look unhealthy. *How did he die?* she wondered.

He was wearing a tuxedo, but not an ordinary one. It looked like there was glittery stuff on the collar and cuffs. And underneath the coat, he wasn't wearing the white shirt and black tie you'd expect to see—he had on a T-shirt. Maybe it was some kind of fashion statement. Or maybe it reflected Rick's sense of humor. He had a great smile, and even though she couldn't actually make out a twinkle in his eyes, she felt very sure it was there.

Normally, Amanda wouldn't find this whole look attractive—she preferred guys who were more manly and athletic in appearance, like Ken. But there was something very appealing about Rick Lasky, something that stirred her.

She looked at Nancy again. Amanda had to admit that she was pretty. Not as pretty as Amanda, of course, but she had a nice face. The gown was awful—all fluffy and puffy—but she could see that Nancy had a good figure. She wore a corsage of roses, which Amanda assumed were red. Naturally, Rick would have given her her favorite flowers to wear.

*It must be a prom picture*, she thought. Was this the prom where Nancy broke up with him?

Now she had a last name, if this really was her Rick in the picture. How funny that she was now thinking of him as "her" Rick. She went to the back of the yearbook and looked up *Lasky, Richard* in the index. There were four page numbers after his name.

The first one directed her to a group photo of some club called *Celestial Turnings*. Reading the caption under the picture, she learned that this was a literary magazine that featured creative writing by students.

She'd always thought students who were in this type of club would be nerds—brainy types who didn't know how to have fun—but these kids didn't look bad at all. Rick looked even cuter than he did in the prom picture.

The next picture was the standard senior class photo—head and shoulders, dark robe with one of those flat tasseled things on his head, fake background of blue sky and clouds. Rick had pulled his hair back into a ponytail for this one, and this gave her a better view of his face. Small ears, high cheekbones, deep-set eyes. Brown, or maybe a very dark blue. Warm, soft eyes. She felt a little flutter in her—in Ken's—stomach.

The third photo was the one taken at the prom. The fourth was the same as the class photo, but enlarged, covering almost the entire page. And bordered in black. Under the picture, she read, "In Memoriam: Richard (Rick) Lasky, 1950–1968."

She remembered he had died during his senior year, just after the prom. An overwhelming sadness came over her, and she felt an almost uncontrollable urge to cry. Which was ridiculous—all this had happened more than 40 years ago. And it wasn't as if she actually knew him—he was just a voice, that was all.

She went back to the computer and entered his name and the school's name into the search box. She was rewarded with an article from the local newspaper. An obituary.

Richard Lasky, age 18, killed in an accident on the highway. He'd been on his brother's motorcycle, she guessed. That was why he didn't like talking about it.

For the longest time, she just stared at the report. Then she went back to the dusty room. On another shelf, she found bound copies of other school publications—directories, newspapers, theater programs. And *Celestial Turnings*.

She searched the issues published between 1965

and 1968 and found two short stories and several poems by Rick. The stories were a little too wordy for her liking, but the poems were nice. One in particular.

It was called "Nancy," and it was a love poem.

*I want to dive into the blue ocean of your eyes*
*And swim to your heart.*
*If you want me to stay, I will live and breathe as part*
*of you and ask for nothing in return.*
*But even if you don't want me to stay, I will not leave.*
*I will simply drown in a sea of my own tears.*

Now she really wanted to cry. To be loved like that—how unbelievably beautiful. Nancy couldn't appreciate this. She didn't deserve him.

*I do*, she thought. She took the magazine to a photocopy machine.

Later that evening, alone in Ken's room, she read the poem over and over again. And each time she read it, she felt it more and more. And she fantasized about someday when a boy would write a poem like that for her . . .

But why fantasize?

She turned on Ken's computer and opened the

word-processing program. Then she retyped Rick's poem, making one change—the title. She printed it out. Then she folded it carefully, put it in an envelope, and on the envelope wrote the name that was now the title of the poem.

*Amanda.*

# CHAPTER TWELVE

JENNA WAS HAVING SUNDAY lunch with her father in a real restaurant, the kind with cloth napkins. "How's your chicken?" Stuart asked her.

"Delicious," she replied. Of course she'd eaten chicken before, many times, but she'd never had it like this, in a sauce with small mushrooms.

Her father was eating some kind of fish. There were a lot of little bones that he had to keep picking out, which would have driven Jenna crazy, but he didn't seem to mind. A man like Stuart Kelley, who had once lived alone on a beach for a month and had fished for his own meals every day, wouldn't be bothered by a few bones. His life had been so amazing!

"Did you really work on an African safari?" she asked him.

"Only for a couple of weeks," he said. "And it

wasn't one of those heavy-duty hunting safaris."

This was something else she liked about him—he didn't brag about everything he'd done. He was matter-of-fact about his adventures.

"Good," Jenna said in relief. "I don't like the idea of killing animals." She looked down at her plate. "I eat them, though. I guess that makes me kind of a hypocrite."

"I feel exactly the same way," Stuart confided, and once again, Jenna had that warm, happy feeling she'd been experiencing a lot lately. They had so much in common!

She had one worry, though. How could a man who'd been living such an exciting life suddenly move here and settle down with a regular job and a family? Because that was now her fantasy, and as hard as she tried to let her natural pessimism and distrust have an impact, the stories kept playing out in her head. A house with a yard. A mother, a father, maybe a dog, maybe even a little brother or sister . . .

"Stu? Stu Kelley?"

A red-faced man in a bright Hawaiian shirt had stopped by their table. Her father rose.

"Arnie! Good to see you!" The two men shook hands.

"What's it been—ten years? More?" the man asked. "How long are you in town for?"

"I'm not sure," Stuart said. He turned and gave Jenna a wink. "Depends on how things work out."

"What are you doing these days?"

"Not much. I'm between jobs at the moment. The money's running out, though, so I have to start looking around."

Once again, Jenna felt a rush of admiration. He didn't have much money, but he'd scraped together enough to take his daughter out to lunch in a restaurant where you didn't have to stand in line at a counter. She made a mental note not to order dessert.

The florid man nodded toward the opposite end of the restaurant. "Well, if you've still got a few bucks and you feel lucky, you might be interested in the back room."

"The back room?"

"There's a regular poker game there every Sunday afternoon. Nice guys, and the stakes aren't too high.

I'm on my way there now. Want to join us?"

"No thanks," Stuart said. "I'm spending the day with my daughter." He introduced them. Stuart and the big man promised each other to stay in touch, and Arnie took off for his game in the back room.

"Is poker a hard game to play?" Jenna asked.

"Not really. It's hard to win, though. It depends a lot on the cards you're dealt, so luck is a major factor. And reading minds."

Jenna's eyes widened. "Reading minds?"

Stuart laughed. "Not literally, Jenna. Have you ever heard the expression *poker face*?"

"No."

"It's when someone's expression tells you nothing about what they're thinking. It comes from the fact that in poker, frequently you have to bluff and pretend your cards are better or worse than they really are so that the other players will bet or raise or fold the way you want them to—so you can win."

She didn't know what he meant by raising or folding, but she got the general idea. "You have to guess what the other people are holding?"

"Exactly. And if the players have good poker faces,

it's not easy. How about some dessert?"

"No thank you," Jenna said properly.

He didn't want any dessert either, so he called for the check, and the waiter brought it to the table. "Now, what would you like to do this afternoon? How about a movie?" He opened his wallet and took out some money. Jenna could see that there was very little left. She tried to think of something they could do that wouldn't cost anything.

"Do you know what I'd really like to do? See a real poker game."

Stuart was surprised. "Why?"

"I like card games, and I want to see how it works."

Stuart smiled. "I'm afraid it's not a spectator sport. Those guys in the back room aren't going to want us watching them."

"What if you played?" Jenna asked. "Would they let me sit with you?"

He looked at her in amusement. "You really want to do that?"

She bobbed her head up and down vigorously. He shrugged.

"We can ask."

In the back room, there was a pool table, a foosball machine, and a couple of tables where people were playing cards. When Arnie looked up and saw Stuart and Jenna, he waved them over.

"Hey, we're just about to start a new round. Want to join in?"

"Do you mind if my kid sits with me?" Stuart asked.

One of the other men grinned. "As long as she's only looking at *your* cards."

Stuart pulled over two chairs and they sat down. Jenna winced as he added what little was left in his wallet to the pot, and the cards were dealt.

Jenna wasn't exactly sure what was going on—all the calling and raising meant nothing to her. But after a while, some things became clear. The cards that a player was holding were called a hand, and the best hand won the game. Sometimes, though, people would pretend to have a better hand than they really did so that the other players would give up. That was the bluffing part.

Only nobody seemed to be bluffing in this game,

and it was all kind of boring. Jenna realized she had made a mistake—card games were only fun when you yourself were playing them. Like her father said, poker wasn't a spectator sport.

She found a magazine in the corner and brought it back to her chair. It was about cars and wasn't any more interesting than the poker game, so once again she indulged in fantasies about her future life. She wondered how her mother would feel about her ex-husband's return. Would she be happy? She never talked about Stuart or expressed any interest or curiosity in where he was or what he was doing. Probably because she thought she'd never see him again. She was in for a big surprise . . .

"Jenna? What do you think?"

She shoved aside her daydreams and turned to her father.

"What?"

"Everyone's folded—it's just me and Mr. Clifford there. What I don't know is whether or not Mr. Clifford has a better hand than I do."

She glanced at her father's hand. It looked pretty good to her—three aces, two kings. But if Mr. Clifford had something like four aces and a king, it didn't matter—Stuart would lose and Mr. Clifford would get that pile of money in the center of the table.

"Take a look at him," her father urged her. "Do you think he's bluffing?"

She looked at the man across the table. He seemed friendly, with bushy eyebrows and a broad smile. She didn't have the slightest idea what kind of cards he had—he held them close, like all the players, and all she could see was the back of them. Too bad she didn't have x-ray vision.

But she did, in a way. Even if she couldn't see the actual cards, Mr. Clifford was probably thinking about them.

She was pretty sure it wasn't the right thing to do, but she couldn't resist. It would be so awful for Stuart to lose the little money he had left. So she did her thing.

And she was right about what was going on in Mr. Clifford's thoughts. There they were, spread out in her mind—two aces, two jacks, and a ten. She didn't know the value for sure, but it seemed to her that her father's hand was stronger.

"I don't think you should fold."

He didn't—he raised the bet, which Jenna thought was crazy, because he didn't have any more money. But then Mr. Clifford had to show his cards, and Stuart won.

Mr. Clifford wasn't angry. He congratulated Stuart and said, "Your daughter's got good instincts."

Stuart nodded. "Yes, I think I'll keep her," he said jovially.

When Jenna saw how much money he'd won, she was pleased. "I'm glad I was right," she told him.

"But you knew you were right, didn't you? You read his mind."

She admitted she had. "But I guess that's cheating, huh? I probably shouldn't have done it."

He laughed. "That's one way to look at it."

She wasn't sure what he meant, but he wasn't mad at her, and that was all that mattered.

He insisted on getting her a little gift with some of his winnings, and she let him buy her a T-shirt—black, of course, with silver glittery stars all over it.

"Thanks," she said. "Have you tried any of those fake tattoos?"

"Not yet. How about you?"

She hesitated. Then, with an abashed smile, she took off her cardigan and revealed her upper right arm, where the word *Dad* was emblazoned in red.

Stuart put an arm around her shoulders and gave her a little squeeze. "That's my girl."

It seemed as though she'd been waiting for a moment like this all her life. Not that she'd been depressed about not having a father—like her mother, she had never given him much thought. But she had one now, and better late than never.

When they got back to the Devons' house, Mrs. Devon insisted that Stuart stay for dinner. While the adults had their cocktails, Jenna ran up to Tracey's room to show off her new T-shirt.

"Guess what?" she said to Tracey. "I'm happy!"

"You should be," Tracey said. "It's a great T-shirt."

Jenna picked up her pillow and tossed it playfully at Tracey. "Not just for that. Tracey, I really think he's going to stay! As soon as my mother comes out of the hospital, he's going to talk to her. And they might get back together!"

"Don't get carried away," Tracey cautioned her.

"Your mother doesn't even know he's back in town. She might not want him."

"Are you crazy?" Jenna shrieked. She threw herself on the bed and gazed at the ceiling. "He's handsome, he's funny, he's nice . . . Who wouldn't want a man like that?"

"He doesn't have a job, does he?"

"He can *get* one. You wouldn't believe all the interesting jobs he's had. He worked on a ship, he worked at a safari camp, he had a job in Alaska—"

"Really? That's what he said?"

Jenna sat up. "You think he's lying?"

"Oh no," Tracey said quickly. "It's just interesting that he's had such a variety of jobs. What did you two do today?"

"We had lunch in a restaurant, and then we played poker. Well, my father played—I just watched. And he won!"

"Lucky him," Tracey said.

"It wasn't luck," Jenna confessed, and she told Tracey about reading the other player's mind.

It probably wasn't the right thing to do—Tracey was big on honesty. Jenna wasn't surprised when

Tracey scolded her.

"That wasn't smart," she said reprovingly. "I'm sure Stuart wouldn't be happy to know you did that."

"He knows," Jenna admitted. "I told him."

Tracey looked at her curiously. "What did he say?"

"He laughed."

Tracey looked appalled. "You're kidding!"

"My father is very cool," Jenna informed her. "He doesn't lecture or give lessons on how to behave."

Tracey murmured something that Jenna couldn't hear.

"What did you say?"

"I just said . . . that doesn't sound very fatherly."

Jenna stared at her. "What's that supposed to mean?"

"Nothing."

But there was an uneasy silence in the air, which Jenna finally broke. "Don't you like my father?"

"He's okay," Tracey said. "It's just that . . ."

"What?"

"Well, he just shows up out of nowhere, says he's

your father, and all of a sudden your whole life is going to change. I just don't want you to be too disappointed."

"Why would I be disappointed?" Jenna asked in bewilderment. Then, something else Tracey had said echoed in her ears. "What do you mean, he *says* he's my father? Don't you *believe* he's my father?"

"I don't know," Tracey replied. "Maybe. But your mother hasn't seen him yet. And you believe him because you can't read his mind. Which isn't much to go on."

"My mother could have been at home when he came to Brookside Towers," Jenna pointed out.

"But she wasn't," Tracey said. "And maybe he knew that."

"That doesn't make any sense," Jenna argued. "Why would he lie about being my father? To hang out with me? He's not some kind of sicko!"

"Oh no, I didn't mean that," Tracey said hastily. "All I'm saying is that you should take it easy. Don't jump to any conclusions."

Jenna glared at her. "I *like* my conclusions."

Tracey was silent. Then she offered Jenna a half

smile. "I'm sorry. I shouldn't talk like that about him—it's none of my business anyway. Let's talk about something else."

"Fine," Jenna said. "What did *you* do today?"

"Practiced disappearing."

"Oh yeah? How did it go?"

"I'm getting better," Tracey told her. "I was able to go completely invisible for a full minute. At least, I *think* I was completely invisible. It's hard to tell, looking in a mirror. There might have been an outline of me or something I didn't see."

"Try it now and I'll tell you if you're invisible," Jenna suggested.

Tracey's brow puckered, and she gazed at Jenna steadily for a moment. "Okay," she said finally. She went over to Jenna's side of the room, by the door. "If I disappear, time me so I'll know how long I can do it." She handed Jenna her cell phone and showed her the stopwatch feature. Then she stepped back a few paces.

Jenna watched. Tracey stood very still with her eyes closed. She breathed evenly and steadily, in a way that told Jenna she was concentrating.

And she began to fade. At first, it was practically imperceptible. Jenna thought it was her own imagination or wishful thinking that made Tracey seem less solid to her. But then she actually began to see through Tracey. She was translucent, and then she was transparent. Jenna couldn't see her at all.

She started the stopwatch. She was still feeling a little annoyed with Tracey for not being enthusiastic about Stuart. But Tracey hadn't had an easy life until now—she'd been ignored at home and tormented at school—so it was probably hard for her to accept people or believe in them. Stuart would work his charm on her eventually.

How long had Tracey been able to stay invisible earlier? A full minute? She'd been gone longer than that already. It was a minute and 19 seconds . . .

A form started to appear, and Jenna stopped the watch. "One minute and twenty-two seconds," she announced as Tracey became solid again. "Why are you so out of breath?"

Tracey was panting, and her fists were clenched. "You think it doesn't take any energy to vanish?"

"I didn't think it was like running a marathon,"

Jenna commented. "Hey, I'm starving. Did your mother put out any of those nibbly things with the cocktails?"

"Go look," Tracey said. "I'll be down soon." She was still breathing a little heavily, and Jenna caught a glimpse of a strange, sort of sickly expression on her face before she turned away.

Clearly, vanishing required a lot more energy and effort than mind reading, Jenna thought as she ran downstairs. On the other hand, invisibility could be a real benefit in playing poker . . .

# Chapter Thirteen

A REN'T YOU GOING TO watch the basketball game with me?" Ken's father called to the person he thought was his son. Amanda paused at the bottom of the stairs. This was sticky. Ken was seriously into sports, and he probably watched all the games on TV with his father. But she'd prefer to be alone in his room and wait for Rick to contact her.

They'd been "talking," or whatever it was, most of the day. Amanda couldn't remember ever having spent an entire Sunday sitting alone in a bedroom doing absolutely nothing, not even leafing through a copy of *Teen Vogue*. But it was so absolutely fantastic to be able to concentrate completely on communicating with Rick without any distractions.

But now Ken's mother was looking at him–her strangely, too. "You *always* watch the Sunday-night basketball game with your father," she said in a worried voice.

Now she was going to start talking about taking him to the doctor again. "Sure, I want to watch the game. I just wanted to go to the bathroom first."

"Why are you going upstairs?" his father asked. "Use the one in the hall."

She hadn't even noticed that there was another bathroom downstairs. She really had to get her act together if she wasn't going to raise any suspicions— especially if she was going to stay inside Ken's body for a while longer. She wasn't in any rush to get out. Not now, not with Rick in her life. She was in love with him.

When she came out of the bathroom, she went into the den and flopped down in the big, fat recliner.

"Hey," Ken's father cried in outrage. "Since when do you take my chair?"

"Just joking around," Amanda said, leaping up.

"What's gotten into you lately, boy?" Ken's father muttered. He picked up the remote control and turned on the TV. Amanda just hoped he wasn't the type who liked to have running commentaries during the game. She was praying that Rick would contact her, and she could pretend to pay attention to the TV. It was easy to figure out which team Ken and his father supported, so mostly she just needed to shout when they scored and growl or mutter when the other team sent a ball through the basket. She thought she could do this and talk to Rick at the same time.

But she didn't hear from him. She tried to keep her mind open, empty, welcoming, but she heard nothing. And she started to worry. Could Rick have figured out that she wasn't really Ken? She'd been trying very hard in their conversations not to sound girlie, but something could have crept in. Her feelings were becoming so strong that she might have given herself away. Fear clutched her heart. What if he never came back?

She waited and waited and tried not to let her despair show. She couldn't have been doing a very good job, though. Ken's father kept glancing in her direction worriedly. Then Ken's mother came in with a plate full of chocolate-chip cookies.

"Your favorite," she announced, putting the plate on the coffee table between the recliner and the sofa where Amanda was sitting. "Don't let your father have any—he's on a diet."

Chocolate-chip cookies were the last thing in the world she was interested in at that moment. She was so nervous that she thought she'd throw up if she took one bite. So when Ken's father made a move toward the plate, she murmured, "I won't tell." At least some cookies would be gone when Mrs. Preston came back.

Rick didn't show up, and by the time the game was over, she was in agony. She kept going over and over the last conversation they'd had that afternoon. She'd been thinking about the Public Gardens, the place Rick and Nancy used to go, and Rick had recited some of his poetry. Had she not been enthusiastic enough? She'd loved the poetry, and while he'd recited it, she'd imagined herself as—well, herself, listening to this sensitive soul express his love for *her*. Maybe she could have expressed her reaction in a better way, because ever since she'd become Ken, this was the longest they'd gone between conversations.

Luckily for her, the favored team lost, so she had an excuse to look unhappy.

"Don't take it so hard," Ken's father said. "Bailey's knee will be better by next week and they'll come back."

"Right," Amanda said, without the slightest idea

who Bailey was. "I'm going to hit the sack—I'm wiped out."

Once again, she got that worried look from Ken's father. It was only ten o'clock, and she doubted Ken went to bed this early. But she couldn't stand it any longer.

She decided she was going to try to contact Rick. She recalled that time in class when Emily had asked Ken if he could contact her father. She couldn't remember if Ken had said he couldn't, or if he just hadn't wanted to.

Up in Ken's room, she turned off the lights and got into bed. Closing her eyes, she visualized the boy she'd seen in the photos and cleared her mind of everything else.

*Rick. Are you there? Can you hear me? Talk to me, Rick.*

She heard nothing.

*Please, Rick. I need to talk to you. I have to tell you something. It's important.*

It was at this moment that she realized she wanted him to know who she really was. It was a big risk. Maybe he'd be horrified to learn he'd been pouring his heart out to a girl. But how could she have a real relationship with him if he thought she was a boy?

*How can I have a real relationship with him if he's dead?* she asked herself. But she didn't have to answer that because suddenly Rick was there, inside her head.

*Hi, Ken.*

*Rick, hi! I'm so glad you're here!*

*Yeah? Well, I am. You said you've got something important to tell me.*

Was she imagining it or was there a distance between them? She wanted to kick herself. Of course there was a distance—he was six feet under or in heaven, or whatever there was after life.

But he felt so very, very close. She couldn't go on lying to him.

*I'm not Ken, Rick.*

*What are you talking about? Of course you're Ken—no one else can hear me.*

*My name is Amanda. I'm inside Ken's body.*

There was no response. She tried to explain.

*I'm what's called a body snatcher. But I occupy bodies only of people I feel sorry for. I was feeling sorry for Ken, because he can't play soccer since he had an accident. And I became him. So that's why I can hear you.*

Should she go into the whole story, about how she had wanted to make Ken ask her out? She was still debating this when Rick spoke.

*Wow! I can't tell you how happy I am to hear this.*

*Why?*

*Because I was getting these feelings for you. The kind of feelings I didn't expect to have for a guy.*

She wondered if he could hear her gasp.

*Really? You mean, like the feelings you had for Nancy?*

*Exactly. The way you understood my poems . . . You really got them, what I was trying to say.*

*I love your poems. I keep pretending they're about me.*

Had she really just said that? It was so not like Amanda to let a boy know how she felt! Amanda played it cool. Amanda played hard to get. She was on a pedestal. A guy had to *work* for her—he couldn't get her affection this easily.

But Rick could. Rick *had*. She didn't care if Rick thought she was too easy, too available.

*They could be about you. My poems. You're better than Nancy. She never had feelings as strong as yours. You're amazing! You feel so deeply, so strongly, for other people that you can* become *them!*

If only he knew how hard she'd tried all her life to avoid caring and feeling for others.

*I know what you look like. I saw your picture in an old yearbook. It's nice, being able to see you in my head while we're talking.*

*I wish I could see you.*

It hit her then that he had no idea what *she* looked like. He didn't know how pretty Amanda Beeson was. He'd fallen for her personality—her attitude and feelings. She was momentarily dumbstruck. Never in a million years would she have thought that those would be qualities a boy would find appealing in her. She was pretty, she was popular—those were the aspects that pulled in the boys. That was how she got attention.

*Do you want me to describe myself?*

*No, that's not important. I feel as if I know you, as if you're imprinted in my heart. That's enough.*

They talked like this for hours, until Amanda started yawning and knew she was going to fall asleep. They made a date to "meet" after school the following day. And she floated away to sleep on what felt like clouds of love.

★ ★ ★

The next morning, before homeroom, she went to her own locker and waited. A few minutes later, Other-Amanda showed up.

"Hi, Ken," she said.

Amanda recognized her own flirty voice. Other-Amanda fiddled with her locker combination but kept her eyes expectantly on Ken. What would Ken say to her at a moment like this?

She didn't care. She had something to give herself.

"I wrote something for you." It was only a little white lie. After all, she *had* typed it.

Other-Amanda looked puzzled. "What did you write? A letter?"

"No. It's a poem. For you."

Now she looked confused. "Why did you write me a poem?"

"To express my feelings." She pulled the envelope from Ken's backpack and handed it to her. Other-Amanda took it gingerly, as if she were afraid it would bite.

"I'll see you in class," Other-Amanda said, taking off.

But she saw Other-Amanda before that. She went to the school library during her study-hall period and saw her at a table in the back, with Katie and Britney. They were looking at a sheet of paper, and they were laughing.

She edged closer, staying behind a bookshelf so that they couldn't see her. Peering through a space between some books, she got a better look at what they were doing.

She couldn't really say she was surprised when she saw that the paper was her poem—Rick's poem. Other-Amanda was making fun of it and encouraging her friends to do the same.

"Is this unreal or what?" she was asking them. "Can you believe I ever wanted to hook up with him?"

"Do you think he's, like, had a nervous breakdown or something?" Britney wondered.

"I don't know and I don't care," Other-Amanda replied. "This makes my skin crawl. It's so, I don't know, *emotional*."

She made it sound like "emotional" was something disgusting.

"'I want to drown in my tears,'" she misquoted in a squeaky voice. "Ew, this is so weird! Who would have thought someone who looked like Ken Preston could be such a dork?"

Amanda was in pain. It literally hurt to hear these words, and not because she was Ken Preston. The words were difficult to hear because she knew this was exactly what she would say if any boy gave her a love poem. Or what she would have said, before Rick.

Thank goodness Rick couldn't see this Other-Amanda. How could she be so shallow, so unfeeling?

Who was she, anyway? Was this the real her, this Other-Amanda she was watching? Or was she the girl inside Ken who was in love with a poet?

Maybe they were one and the same. Maybe Amanda or Other-Amanda or whoever the real person was just talked like that to impress her friends. Because it was the way *they* behaved. No, she couldn't blame her friends. It was the way *she* behaved. Because she was "cool."

At least Rick would never know this girl. He could talk only through Ken. But she had to go back inside herself sooner or later. That girl over there, making fun of a guy who showed his feelings—that was *her*.

For the first time in her life, she didn't like herself very much.

# CHAPTER FOURTEEN

THERE WAS A SURPRISE waiting for Jenna
after school on Monday. Just as she and Tracey
emerged from the building, she spotted the
now-familiar yellow car at the curb.

"It's my father," she cried in delight. She ran over to
the car.

Stuart rolled down the window. "How's my girl?"

"Fantastic!" Even as she said the word, Jenna was
thinking that this was probably the first time she'd ever
responded to a question about herself with that word.
On the other hand, who had ever called her "my girl"
before?

"Just thought you might be interested in an
afterschool snack," he said.

"Sure!" She waved to Tracey. "C'mon, my dad's
taking us out for something to eat." She was pleased—
this was the perfect opportunity for Tracey to get to

know Stuart and see for herself what a great person he was.

Tracey seemed to be walking unusually slowly, and she didn't look particularly thrilled at the notion.

"Jenna," her father called, beckoning for her to come closer to the window. When she did, he spoke quietly. "Listen, I'd rather this was just the two of us, okay? I need to talk to you."

He looked unusually serious, and at first she was puzzled. Then a disturbing thought occurred to her, and the pessimism she'd pushed to the back of her head returned to the forefront. He wanted to talk to her alone. Why? Because he'd changed his mind about hanging around. Because he was leaving town and he wanted to say goodbye.

She looked back at Tracey. Her friend couldn't have heard him, but she'd stopped approaching anyway.

"Thanks, but I've got tons of homework," Tracey said. "I need to go straight home. Have fun." She turned away and walked off in the opposite direction.

Jenna frowned. Tracey could at least have said hello to Stuart. It wasn't like her to be rude. Jenna joined her father in the car and they headed off. Already depressed, she watched him, waiting for the bad news. She should have known her fantasies were just that—fantasies. Ex-husbands and wives didn't reunite after 13 years—not when they hadn't had any contact at all during that time. There wasn't going to be any little house with a backyard. All those silly dreams she'd had were going to stay just that, dreams. Her father was going to leave, and another 13 years might pass before she'd see him again.

She pressed her lips together tightly. She would *not* cry. At least, not in front of him. After all the experiences in her life, why hadn't she learned that people always ended up letting you down? She wanted to be angry. But all she could feel was this enormous sense of disappointment.

Stuart pulled into a fast-food restaurant and ordered a couple of drinks from the drive-through window. "Want something to eat?" he asked her. "Some fries? A burger?"

"No thank you," she said stiffly. Five minutes ago, she'd been hungry. Now food was the last thing on her mind. Without a word, she took the drink he handed her. They left the parking lot, and he drove silently for a couple of minutes. Turning down a pretty street lined with trees and cute bungalows, he pulled alongside the curb and stopped. As he turned off the engine, Jenna asked, "What are we doing here?"

He didn't answer the question. "There's something I have to tell you," he said.

Jenna looked out the window on her side so that she wouldn't have to face him as she replied. "I know. You're leaving."

His silence confirmed her suspicions. Then he said, "I want to explain . . ."

She interrupted. "You don't have to. Could you just take me back to Tracey's?"

"Only if you're willing to leave tomorrow."

Slowly, she turned toward him. "What?"

"Listen to my plan," he said. "I'm tired of running around, and I want to settle down. And I want to make up for what I did to you and your mother. But I'm not doing this just because I feel guilty."

Jenna was more confused than ever. "Doing what?"

He took a sip of his drink before responding.

"I saw your mother this morning."

She was completely taken aback. "How? She's not

allowed to have any visitors."

He grinned. "You might not have noticed this, but your father can be pretty charming. I had a little talk with one of the nurses, and she bent the rules."

Jenna was surprised. She thought hospitals were pretty strict about regulations. "How's she doing? Was she shocked to see you?"

"Very. But happy, I'm glad to say. And she looks wonderful. This treatment is working."

"That's great." With no idea what was coming next, Jenna waited uncertainly.

"She'll be leaving the hospital on Sunday," he continued. "And I don't want either of you living in that apartment anymore. I'm going to buy a house."

She blinked. "A house? For me and Mom?"

"For all three of us. To live together, as a family."

Jenna couldn't speak. The lump in her throat was almost painful, and at the same time, she'd never felt so happy.

"Your mother is going to give me another chance," he said. "I don't deserve it, but she wants this, too. I hope you feel the same way."

She felt pretty sure that her expression answered

for her. But just in case, she said, "Oh, I do. I do."

He smiled. "Good. Now, we have to be practical. I don't want us spending even one night at Brookside Towers. This morning I saw a house I want to buy." He leaned across Jenna and pointed. "What do you think of it?"

It was like the house of her fantasies. White, with blue trim. Boxes at the windows spilling out red geraniums. Big hanging baskets of flowers on each side of the front door. A manicured lawn. It wasn't a mansion, or even a large house like the Devons'. It was cozy and sweet. It wasn't just a house—it was a home. The perfect little home for a family of three.

"It's beautiful," she breathed.

"I wish you could see the inside, but the owners are out for the day."

"Are you sure it's for sale?" she asked. "I don't see any sign."

"They're nice people," he told her. "Even though I couldn't give them any money up front, they took down the sign. I have until Friday to pay them."

"Friday," she repeated. "This Friday? You mean this week?"

"Yes."

She was mystified. "But it must cost thousands and thousands of dollars. How are you going to get that kind of money? Can you borrow it from the bank?"

He smiled ruefully. "Not with my credit history. No, honey, I'm going to pay cash. And I'm hoping you'll help me."

"How?"

"I'm going to get a few bucks together today and tomorrow," he told her. "Enough for a couple of plane tickets and a little more. On Wednesday, you and I could fly to Las Vegas. The casinos there are open twenty-four hours a day. I could join a poker game, and with you by my side, I could win the cost of that house by Friday morning. We fly back, I hand the folks the money, we move in on Saturday. We pick up your mother on Sunday and bring her home. Here."

He'd completely taken her breath away. She wasn't even sure she'd comprehended what he'd just said.

"Do you think you can handle it?" he asked. "Staying up all night reading minds?"

"I don't know. I guess."

"Of course you can—you're a tough cookie.

You're my girl, right?"

"Right." It wasn't the staying up all night that was bothering her, though. "But . . ."

"But what?"

She made a little face. "We'd be cheating." Deep inside she knew it was wrong.

He didn't disagree. "Yes, you're right. And as a father, I suppose I should be ashamed of myself, asking my daughter to help me cheat. But I'm looking at the big picture, Jenna. I'm thinking about saving your mother, making us all happy. Being a real family. It would take years and years for me to save up the money for this house. I don't think your mother can last years and years at that place where you've been living."

He was right, and she knew that. Brookside Towers was no place for a recovering alcoholic. There was just too much temptation to go back to her old ways.

"Do you know the expression 'The end justifies the means'?" he asked her.

She shook her head.

"It means that sometimes you have to do things that aren't one hundred percent right in order to reach a goal that's more important. We're talking about your mother's health and our future as a family. Don't you think it's worth doing something a little unethical for that?"

She still didn't feel good about it, but he was right. "Yes."

He leaned over and gave her a quick hug. "Excellent. I'll call your principal tomorrow and make arrangements to take you out of school on Wednesday."

"I think you'd better come up with a different reason for it," she cautioned him.

He chuckled. "Not to worry, Jenna. Your old man can spin a tale. I'll say you've got a sick grandmother who wants to see you. We can use the same line with the Devons."

"Okay."

He started up the car. "Now, I have to go scrape together the money for our tickets and enough for me to get into a game. I'll drop you off at the Devons'."

It wasn't far. When they moved into this house, she'd still be in the same school zone. As he drove, Stuart talked about job possibilities for him in the town, but Jenna was in too much of a fog to listen.

It was happening. It was really happening. Her dreams, her fantasies—they were going to come true. Like in a fairy tale. She had no idea something like this could happen in real life.

At the Devons' house, he gave her a quick kiss on the forehead and told her that he'd let her know what time they'd be leaving on Wednesday. Still feeling dazed, Jenna went inside.

"I'm in the kitchen," Tracey called out.

"I'll be there in a minute," Jenna called back. First, she needed a little time alone. She ran up the stairs to Tracey's room.

It was a funny thing about emotions, she thought. They never seemed to be precise—at least, hers weren't. She was never 100 percent happy or 100 percent miserable. Right now, for example, she'd just heard the best news she'd ever heard in her life. She should have been ecstatic.

Okay, so she'd have to do something she really didn't like doing, but so what? She just had to keep telling herself what Stuart had said about the ends and the means. And it wasn't as if she was so virtuous about her gift anyway. She'd certainly read minds for more stupid reasons than this! Madame was always scolding her for eavesdropping on people's thoughts.

She wasn't sure how the Devons would react, though. They were responsible for her, as her foster family. They might not want her flying off to Las Vegas, even if they believed it was to see a sick grandmother. They might want to get permission from social services, and then it would turn into a big deal. Stuart would have to fill out forms—there would be little chance they could get permission by Wednesday. Which would mean they wouldn't have the money for the house on Friday. Which would mean her mother would come out of the rehab program on Sunday and go straight back to Brookside Towers.

Jenna had an idea. Instead of telling them, she'd leave them a note that they'd find only after she'd gone. Tracey would be furious with her for not telling her the truth, but when she saw how happy Jenna was in her new home with her new family, she'd have to forgive her.

Jenna needed paper. Tracey kept school supplies in a cabinet under her desk, and Jenna found a pad there. Then she opened the drawer to get something to write with.

Her eyes fell on an envelope, sealed, addressed, and apparently waiting for a stamp so that it could be mailed. *That's odd*, she thought. Tracey was a big e-mailer; she never wrote old-fashioned letters.

But this looked like something official. Jenna knew she was being nosy—it was none of her business—but so what? If she could read minds, she could look at envelopes. And it wasn't as if she was going to open it.

She picked it up and examined the address. *State Medical Laboratories. Department of DNA Testing.*

Was Tracey writing a paper about DNA? She hadn't mentioned it.

Jenna heard footsteps and dropped the envelope onto the desk. Tracey came in.

"I'm bringing the kitchen to you," she announced. In her hand was a plate of brownies. "I just made these. You're probably not hungry, though, if you just had something to eat with Stuart."

"I'm starving," Jenna said, taking a brownie. Sitting on her bed, she hoped Tracey wouldn't notice that an envelope that had been in her drawer was now on top of her desk.

Tracey did notice, but she must have thought she'd left it there herself, because she just picked it up and opened her drawer to slide it back in. That was when Jenna read her mind. She couldn't resist it. There was something furtive about Tracey's movements, something that made Jenna think she didn't want her to know about this envelope.

And for a good reason. As she was handling the envelope, Tracey thought about it, and her mind revealed what was contained inside.

Hairs. Some of Jenna's that Tracey had gathered from her hairbrush. And some that belonged to Stuart.

Tracey had plucked them from his head when she had been invisible the day before. That was why she'd been out of breath when she became visible again, just more than a minute later. During that time, she had run downstairs, pulled the hairs from an unsuspecting Stuart while he sipped his cocktail with the Devons, and hurried back to her room.

Jenna wondered if he'd felt it and what he'd thought it could have been. A mosquito?

Of course, that wasn't really relevant or important. What was important was the fact that Tracey was so convinced that Stuart wasn't Jenna's father that she was willing to take the extreme measure of having their DNA compared to see if they were actually related.

Automatically, Jenna reached for another brownie. She had to keep in motion, keep busy, so she wouldn't reveal what she knew to Tracey. At least, not until she'd figured out what she was going to do about it.

"They're good, aren't they?"

Jenna looked at Tracey blankly. "Huh?"

"The brownies. I've got another batch in the oven. In fact, I'd better go check on them." Tracey left the room. As soon as she was gone, Jenna went to the drawer. Opening it, she retrieved the envelope and went into the bathroom. There, she tore the letter up, again and again, into little tiny pieces that wouldn't clog the plumbing. Then she dropped them into the toilet and flushed it.

She'd have to find some way to tell her father that he should let her know if he ever felt anything unusual, like a mosquito bite out of season—without telling him why.

# Chapter Fifteen

O KAY, THAT'S IT," MRS. Preston said. "I'm calling the doctor." Amanda looked up. "Why?"

"Because you haven't said a word since we sat down to dinner. Not to mention the fact that it's your favorite, lasagna, and you've barely touched it." The woman got up from the table and went to the phone.

Hastily, Amanda dug her fork into the lasagna. "I'm eating!" she yelled.

"Too late," Ken's mother called back. "Something's wrong with you, and I'm going to find out what it is." A moment later, she reappeared. "The doctor's office is closed. But I'm calling again first thing in the morning."

Amanda couldn't worry about that now. She had bigger things on her mind. Like raising the dead.

Not like in the movies, when zombies came up from the ground and vampires emerged from coffins.

Just making someone dead be alive again, as he was before.

She wasn't stupid, and she didn't believe in magic or reincarnation, or anything like that. But look at her—she could take over bodies. That wasn't scientific—nobody could explain it. The same was true of every student in her gifted class. They could all do inexplicable things. Reading minds, seeing the future, making things move on their own—none of these skills made any sense in a logical world. So maybe one of them could bring the dead back to life but just didn't know it yet. Why not? It wasn't any freakier than anything else they did. The question was—who would be a likely candidate? Whose gifts might extend to something like that?

During her "date" with Rick that evening, she didn't mention her plan. She let the conversation go on in its usual lovely way. Rick talked about his dreams, goals, and ambitions—things that could never come true now that he was dead. He didn't sound depressed, though, and she soon found out why.

She asked a question that had been in the back of her mind since they'd met.

*What's it like, where you are?*

*Beautiful.*

*Can you tell me about it?*

*It's hard to describe. It's just this incredibly happy place,*
*full of love.*

*I'd like to see it.*

*You will, someday. Not for a long time, though, I*
*think. You're not the type to get into a stupid motorcycle*
*accident. And you have to wait till it's your time or you*
*won't come here.*

She understood. Not that she was thinking of
trying to get there on her own, to be with him. No,
she wanted him *here*, in her world. As beautiful as his
world might be, she preferred to stay alive for the
time being.

So they talked about other things. She confessed
that she hadn't given much thought to her own
future. He talked about college. He'd never been, of
course, but his older brother had loved it. He told her
he thought she'd make a wonderful teacher because
she expressed herself so well. Nobody had ever told
her that before, mostly because it hadn't been true.

She told him about her family, about being an

only child, and how spoiled she was as the center of attention in her real home. She described her other experiences as a body snatcher.

She left out a lot of stuff about her life, too. She didn't talk about her clique—how they always sat together at lunch and criticized other girls. She didn't tell him how frequently she went shopping for clothes and makeup, shoes, and hair products.

He talked about books he'd read when he was alive. He'd been a big reader. A couple of titles were familiar, but only because they'd been required reading for a class, and even then, she'd used only the CliffsNotes so that she wouldn't have to waste valuable television time reading. She didn't know most of the books he mentioned, but she filed the titles away in her memory for future reading. This dead guy was going to change the way she lived. And maybe, just maybe, he wouldn't have to stay dead.

In her gifted class the next day, Other-Amanda was giving her report on how her gift could influence her career choice. Real Amanda had lucked out—she wouldn't have to do it. Of course, sooner or later Ken would have to give *his* report.

Other-Amanda didn't surprise her. Amanda knew herself too well.

"I don't think there's anything positive about my gift at all, and it can't do me any good in the future. I want to have a fabulous life, and I can't have that if I can transfer only into bodies I feel sorry for. So my goal is to lose my gift, and that will help me achieve my goals."

"Which are?" Madame inquired.

"If I grow a few more inches, I could be a model. If I don't grow, I suppose I could be a movie star."

"Do you enjoy acting?" the teacher asked.

"I don't know—I've never tried it."

"You're not in the drama club here at school?"

Other-Amanda rolled her eyes. "No. They're not my kind of people."

Amanda-Ken saw something that Other-Amanda wouldn't have noticed—the way her classmates were looking at her. Emily and Tracey were exchanging exasperated looks. Sarah was shaking her head sadly. Jenna seemed preoccupied, as if she wasn't even listening to the report, but Martin and Charles were whispering, and they were both looking at Other-Amanda with expressions that weren't pleasant.

Ken probably looked the way she was feeling. Disgusted. With herself.

As Other-Amanda continued with her life goals, which essentially involved being rich and beautiful and having fun all the time, Amanda-Ken looked around the room and wondered who might be capable of bringing Rick back. It seemed to her that Sarah was the most likely candidate. At least, she had the most powerful gift, even if she refused to use it. Amanda would have to talk to her . . .

*What do you think, Rick? There's a girl who can make people do things, even if they don't want to. I'm wondering if maybe she's got gifts that she doesn't know she has.*

*Like what?*

*Bringing someone back. From where you are. So we could be together.*

There was no response.

*Rick?*

*I'm here. I'm listening.*

*I'd probably have to tell her the whole story, about being Ken right now, and falling in love with you . . .*

She caught herself. Had she actually used that word before, with him? Was she coming on too strong?

*It won't do any good.*

*Why?*

*Because it can't happen. That kind of power doesn't exist. Not outside movies and stories.*

*But I can't stay inside Ken forever! His parents think he's sick—his mother's taking me to the doctor tomorrow. I don't know how or when I'll get back inside myself, but it's going to happen sooner or later.*

*I know.*

*Then what are we going to do? Once I'm myself again, we won't even be able to talk!*

*I know.*

*That's the second time you've said that! Don't you have any ideas?*

*Only one. We have to stop connecting. Now.*

She must have gasped audibly, because everyone in the class was looking at her.

"Ken? Are you all right?"

"Um, I'm feeling nauseous. Can I be excused?"

Madame quickly handed Amanda-Ken a hall pass, and she hurried out of the room. She ran down two flights to the basement restroom that nobody used, the one where she always went when she needed complete privacy.

*Okay, I'm back. Why do we have to stop connecting now? Don't you have feelings for me?*

*Of course I do. That's why we have to stop. Because it's going to get only more difficult for both of us.*

*But that's not fair! Not if you love me and I love you!*

*It's not fair to die in a motorcycle accident when you're eighteen years old. It's not fair that people are hungry. It's not fair that a bad person can succeed and a good person fails.*

*I don't care about anyone else—I'm talking about us!*

*You don't mean what you just said. Of course you care about other people. You're that kind of person.*

Was she? She wasn't so sure.

*I don't want to lose you!*

*I'll be in your memory. You'll be in mine.*

*That's not enough. I want more.*

*Oh, Amanda, you can't have it all. You must know that.*

But she didn't know that. She'd always had everything she wanted, and she wasn't about to stop now. Not when she'd found someone she wanted to be with more than anyone else in the world. This couldn't be happening to her, Amanda Beeson! She would *not* allow her heart to break! They belonged together, she and Rick. They had to be together . . .

But from some place far away, in the deepest recesses of her mind, she heard a faint voice.

*Goodbye, my love.*

And she wasn't in the restroom anymore.

She was in her seat in the gifted class. Her usual seat—Amanda's seat. Madame was looking at her with interest. Amanda didn't think it was because of her report.

But all Madame said was, "Thank you, Amanda. Sarah, would you like to go next?"

Amanda didn't hear a word Sarah said. Her head was spinning and she was trying to get a grip on herself.

How did she get here? Was it the strength of her emotions that had pushed her back inside her own body? Emotions she'd never admitted to herself before?

The classroom door opened and a dazed-looking Ken entered.

"Feeling better?" Madame asked, eyeing him keenly.

He nodded and took his seat. He glanced at

Amanda and then looked quickly away.

*He's embarrassed*, Amanda thought. *He knows I was using him and he's feeling awkward. Not to mention the fact that he came to in a girls' restroom.*

She waited for the bell to ring and went to his seat before he could even get up.

"Hi . . ." she said, uncertain as to how he would respond.

He finally looked directly at her. "What happened?"

So he knew he hadn't been himself and he knew she had something to do with it. She realized honesty was the only way to go.

"I was inside your body. I saw you watching the soccer team practice. You looked so sad, and I felt sorry for you, and then, well, it just happened."

Okay, she wasn't being *completely* honest. But he didn't have to know her real motives. Mostly because those motives had disappeared once Rick had come into her life.

"How did it feel?" she asked. "Having me inside you?"

"I don't know," he said. "I mean, it was like a dream, all blurry and . . . and not real. Like I was here and I wasn't here . . ." He looked at her helplessly.

She could almost understand how he felt. It had to be so personal, having someone else inside you. Funny how she had never considered what Tracey felt when she had left *her* body. But then, Amanda Beeson didn't ever consider other people's feelings.

"What did you make me do?" he asked suddenly.

"You gave me a poem," she admitted. Even as she spoke, she knew it was a mistake to tell him this. Because, of course, there was only one thing he could say.

"Why?"

She confessed, "I wanted you to like me."

It wasn't a very flattering reaction. He looked confused and then embarrassed again. He also seemed curious.

"Was it a good poem?" he asked.

"Yeah. But I didn't appreciate it."

He nodded and then rose. "I have to go."

She watched him leave and wondered if she'd ever have any kind of relationship with him again. Of course he wasn't surprised to learn that she hadn't appreciated a poem. The Amanda Beeson he knew wouldn't care.

If she'd known then what she knew now—about people and feelings. About herself. About pain and hurt and sadness.

But now she understood. And like the old poster proclaimed, this could be the first day of the rest of her life. She could be a different person, a better person.

Without Rick. And she had to call on the resources of the old Amanda, the Amanda who didn't care, to keep herself from bursting into tears right there and then.

Because she didn't think the memory would be enough.

# Chapter Sixteen

SOMETHING WEIRD WAS GOING on with Amanda, Jenna thought as she half listened to Sarah's report. She could tell, just from the snotty girl's expression. She could explore her mind and find out what was happening.

But she had too many other things to think about. She was excited and she was scared.

Her father had called the principal to get her excused. He was picking her up right after this class, in less than 30 minutes. They'd be going directly to the airport, where he'd return the little rental car and they'd board a flight to Las Vegas. That was the exciting part.

She hadn't told Tracey, and she hadn't left a note for the Devons. But that wasn't the scary part. She wasn't sure what the scary part was. Flying for the first time? She didn't *think* that was it.

Sarah had finished her report, and Madame called

on Ken. Ken was reluctant.

"Could I put this off till tomorrow?" he asked. "I'm kind of not in the mood."

That wasn't the sort of excuse that Madame usually accepted, but for some strange reason, she smiled at Ken and nodded. "Yes, that's all right. Let's see . . . has everyone given their reports?"

Emily's hand shot up. Madame looked puzzled.

"You gave your report last week, Emily."

"I just have a question to ask Ken, Madame. I was wondering if maybe he's had a chance to think about what I asked him. If he could contact my father."

Madame frowned. "Emily—"

But before she could go on, Amanda spoke.

"Knock it off, Emily! Leave him alone!"

Jenna was stunned, and she assumed that everyone else in the room was having the same reaction. This wasn't like Amanda. She was way too emotional.

And she didn't stop. "You don't know what it's like for Ken—to get involved with people like this, people he can't see or do anything for. It's hard enough for him to cope with the ones who contact him—he shouldn't have to go out and seek them. He suffers. Don't you understand that?"

Was there another body snatcher around? Jenna wondered. Had someone taken over Amanda? She'd never heard Amanda speak with such passion before, not even about herself.

Ken was looking at Amanda, but he didn't seem quite as shocked as everyone else. And strangely enough, Madame was almost smiling.

Suddenly, Ken clutched his head. Madame looked at him in alarm. "Are you all right, Ken?" she asked for the second time that day.

"I'm getting a message," Ken blurted out.

"From my father?" Emily asked excitedly.

"No." He turned to Jenna. "From yours."

Jenna stared at him. "My father isn't dead."

Ken held up one hand and rubbed his forehead with the other. "Wait . . . yes. Okay. I will."

No one had ever actually seen or heard Ken talk to dead people before. The room was hushed and expectant.

His face cleared, and he spoke to Jenna. "He died eight years ago, Jenna. From a gunshot wound, in a fight. He wants me to give you a message."

"This is crazy," Jenna declared hotly. "I don't know who's talking to you, Ken, but it's not my father. Stuart Kelley is alive and well, and he's picking me up in less than thirty minutes."

"He's an impostor," Ken told her. "Your father says that guy found out about you, but he doesn't know how. He's a professional gambler. He wants to use you for your mind-reading gift so he can win at poker."

"That's not true! He saw my mother at the hospital. She'd know if he was an impostor."

"Are you sure he saw your mother, Jenna?" Madame asked quietly.

Amanda reached inside her handbag. "Here, use my cell phone. Call the hospital and find out if she's had any visitors."

"No!" Jenna cried out.

Ken was rubbing his head again. "He's a scam artist, Jenna. He's got a friend working with him. Someone named Arnie. Have you ever heard of him?"

Arnie. The guy in the restaurant who knew him from way back when. The poker game in the back room. Jenna's stomach turned over.

"This isn't true!" she screamed. But it came out as a whisper.

"Your father, your real father—he wants to save you from him, Jenna," Ken told her. "He's trying to protect you. He's had a hard time reaching me, but he wouldn't give up."

Jenna burst into tears.

She couldn't remember the last time she'd done this. Jenna Kelley didn't cry. That's what she'd told Emily when Emily had made that prediction about the tall, dark, handsome stranger. Who gave off bad vibes. Who would make her cry.

Tracey came over and hugged her. Jenna didn't pull away. She was aware of other people leaving their seats, coming over to her, surrounding her. Even Charles wheeled himself over. Madame came, too. Only Carter Street remained in his seat, oblivious to what was going on as usual.

Everyone else made a wall of support around her, keeping her safe, keeping her strong. Still, she couldn't stop crying.

She buried her face in her hands. "It's okay," came

a soft voice. "Let it out." It sounded like Amanda, but of course that was impossible.

Slowly, the tears began to subside, and she could hear Madame's voice over them. "This is why we have to watch out for one another. People will try to use us. And who knows what this man really wants? He could be part of something bigger, some conspiracy. We are always in danger from the outside world, class. What's happened to Jenna—it's a lesson for all of us. We're in this together."

"Why couldn't I read his mind?" Jenna asked in a whisper.

"Who knows?" Madame said simply. "He might have gifts of his own."

"And how could he have known that my mother wouldn't be home when he came to my apartment?"

Madame gently touched her head. "As I said, Jenna, other people could be involved."

Charles spoke. "What a jerk! Hey, Jenna, do you want me to drop a house on him?"

"I'm getting the feeling," Martin said excitedly. "I could go beat him up."

Jenna took her hands away from her wet face.

Tracey silently passed her a tissue.

"It's okay," she said, her voice trembling. "I can handle this myself."

"No, Jenna," Madame said. "We need one another."

The bell rang. Jenna looked at Madame. "He's picking me up in front of the school."

Madame nodded. She made a gesture, and everyone moved away, giving her room to stand up. Carter Street walked out of the room. Everyone else waited around Jenna. When she started to move toward the door, they encircled her, walking with her. Charles rolled along by her side.

Outside, the little yellow compact was waiting by the curb. The circle parted, letting Jenna see the car clearly. And the driver.

The handsome man was smiling. There was no question about it—he had a charming smile. It felt like a knife stabbing her in the heart.

Their eyes met. She still couldn't read his mind, but maybe he read hers. Or maybe it was just written all over her face.

His smile faded. She could see his hand go to the

gearshift. Then, suddenly, he sped away.

Dimly, Jenna heard Madame suggesting to Tracey that she take her home. Emily was saying she'd wait with Jenna while Tracey collected their things. She was aware of a hug, a pat on the shoulder, a hand briefly clutching hers. She wasn't sure who was hugging, who was patting . . . but they were friends, she thought. Maybe.

The only thing she was really sure of was the fake tattoo on her arm. *Dad*. It was already starting to fade. She'd just have to wear long sleeves until it was gone completely.

NINE SECRET GIFTS IN ONE CLASS—
WHAT COULD POSSIBLY GO WRONG?

Find out in an excerpt
from Book 1 in the GIFTED series:

# GIFTED
## OUT OF SIGHT,
## OUT OF MIND

# CHAPTER ONE

THERE WERE 342 STUDENTS at Meadowbrook Middle School and three lunch periods each day. This meant that during any one lunch period there could be no more than 114 students in the cafeteria. The noise and commotion, however, suggested that half the population of mainland China was eating lunch together.

Students roamed the cavernous space, shouting, racing from one end to the other, knocking over chairs, banging trays down on tables. There were a couple of teachers who were supposed to be supervising the scene and maintaining order, but they couldn't stop the occasional flying meatball from that day's Spaghetti Special or the far-reaching spray from a soda bottle that had been intentionally shaken before being opened.

From her prime seat at the best table, Amanda Beeson surveyed the chaotic scene with a sense of well-being. The cafeteria was noisy and messy and not very attractive, but it was part of her little kingdom— or queendom, if such a word existed. She wasn't wearing any kind of crown, of course, but she felt secure in the knowledge that in this particular hive, she was generally acknowledged as the queen bee.

On either side of her sat two princesses—Sophie Greene and Britney Teller. The three of them were about to begin their daily assessment of classmates. As always, Amanda kicked off the conversation. "Ohmigod, check out Caroline's sweater! It's way too tight."

"No kidding," Sophie said. "It's like she's begging for the boys to look at her."

"And it's not like she's got anything on top to look *at*," Britney added.

Amanda looked around for more victims. "Someone should tell Shannon Fields that girls with fat knees shouldn't wear short skirts."

"Terri Boyd has a new bag," Britney pointed out.

"Is it a Coach?"

Amanda shook her head. "No way. It's a fake."

"How can you tell from this far away?" Sophie wanted to know.

Amanda gave her a withering look. "Oh, puh-leeze! Coach doesn't make hobo bags in that shade of green." Spotting imitation designer goods was a favorite game, and Amanda surveyed the crowd for another example. "Look at Cara Winters's sweater."

"Juicy Couture?" Sophie wondered.

"*Not.* You can tell by the buttons."

Sophie gazed at her with admiration. Amanda responded by looking pointedly at the item in Sophie's hand. "Sophie, are you actually going to eat that cupcake? I thought you were on a diet."

Sophie sighed and pushed the cupcake to the edge of her tray. Amanda turned to her other side.

"Why are you staring at me like that?" Britney asked.

"You've got a major zit coming out on your chin."

Britney whipped a mirror out of her bag.

"It's not that big," Sophie assured her. "No one

can see it."

"*I* can," Amanda declared.

"Really?" Britney stared harder into the mirror. Amanda thought she saw her lower lip tremble, and for a moment she almost felt sorry for her. Everyone knew that Britney was obsessed with her complexion. She was constantly searching her reflection for any evidence of an imminent breakout, she spent half her allowance on face creams, and she even saw a dermatologist once a month. Not that she really needed to give her skin all that attention. If Britney's face had been half as bad as she thought it was, she wouldn't be sitting at Amanda's table. But she was still staring into her little mirror, and now Amanda could see her eyes getting watery.

*Oh no, don't let her* cry, she thought. Amanda didn't like public displays of emotion. She was always afraid that she'd get caught up in them herself.

Three more of their friends—Emma, Katie, and Nina—joined them at the table, and Britney got more reassurance on the state of her skin. Finally, Amanda gave in. "You know, I think there's a smudge on one of my contact lenses. Everybody looks like they've got zits."

Britney looked relieved, and Amanda made a mental note not to waste insults on friends. She didn't want to have to feel bad about anything she said. Feelings could be so dangerous.

Luckily, Emma brought up a new subject. "Heather Todd got a haircut."

"From Budget Scissors," Amanda declared, referring to a chain of cheap hair whackers.

"Really?"

"That's what it looks like."

Katie giggled. "Amanda, you're terrible!"

Amanda knew this was intended as a compliment, and she accepted it by smiling graciously. Katie beamed in the aura of the smile, and Amanda decided not to mention the fact that Katie's tinted lip-gloss had smeared.

Besides, there were so many others who were more deserving of her critical attention. Like the girl who was walking toward their table right now: Tracey Devon, the dreariest girl in the eighth grade, the most pathetic creature in the entire class—maybe even in the whole school.

# Gifted by Marilyn Kaye

Nine teenagers. Nine Secrets. Nine powers that can change the world.

Now available:

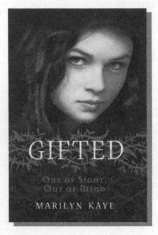

## OUT OF SIGHT, OUT OF MIND

One morning Amanda looked in the mirror and another girl looked back.

## BETTER LATE THAN NEVER

Jenna can read anyone mind, but her long-lost is a total mystery.

Also look out for:

## HERE TODAY, GONE TOMORROW

Emily can see into the future, but her visions show nothing but trouble.

# Traces by Malcolm Rose

When there's a crime to solve, sixteen-year-old forensic investigator, Luke, and his right-hand robot, Malc, are the first ones on the case.

BLOOD BROTHER

DOUBLE CHECK

FINAL LAP

FRAMED!

LOST BULLET

ROLL CALL

## SHORT STORY COLLECTIONS

Great writers, gripping stories, and abundant genres—Kingfisher's short story collections have something for everyone.

MYSTIFYING: SINISTER STORIES
OF THE UNEXPLAINED
Chosen by Helen Cresswell

OUT OF THIS WORLD:
SCIENCE-FICTION STORIES
Chosen by Edward Blishen

PIROUETTE: BALLET STORIES
Chosen by Harriet Castor